T0149464

Books Published by Dennis McKay

Novels:

Fallow's Field – 2007
Once Upon Wisconsin – 2009
A Boy From Bethesda – 2013
The Shaman and the Stranger – 2015
The Accidental Philanderer – 2015

Nonfiction:

Terrapin Tales – 2016 – coauthor Scott McBrien

A Girl From
Bethesda

Dennis McKay

A GIRL FROM BETHESDA

iUniverse books may be ordered through booksellers or by contacting:

iUniverse
1663 Liberty Drive
Bloomington, IN 47403
www.iuniverse.com
1-800-Authors (1-800-288-4677)

Because of the dynamic nature of the Internet, any web addresses or links contained in this book may have changed since publication and may no longer be valid. The views expressed in this work are solely those of the author and do not necessarily reflect the views of the publisher, and the publisher hereby disclaims any responsibility for them.

Any people depicted in stock imagery provided by Thinkstock are models, and such images are being used for illustrative purposes only.
Certain stock imagery © Thinkstock.

ISBN: 978-1-5320-2060-5 (sc)
ISBN: 978-1-5320-2059-9 (e)

Library of Congress Control Number: 2017905009

Print information available on the last page.

iUniverse rev. date: 04/26/2017

Acknowledgment

Book cover design by Megan Belford.

PART 1

Once in a Lifetime

CHAPTER 1

1976

The Endless Summer, or the End, as the locals called it, was a neat little joint in Manhassa Beach—teak bar with a barrel of peanuts at each end, a mural of surfers in various stages from paddling out past the break to hanging ten inside a tube, and a Wurlitzer tucked in a corner playing songs from the fifties and sixties. The place had an upscale, shabby let-it-all-hang-out sort of feel. It was Bo Ricker's kind of place. He enjoyed the energy of the joint—the young, raucous crowd; the sounds and smells of the ocean; and the freedom of it all.

At the waitress station was Bo's girlfriend, wearing jean shorts and a yellow T-shirt, on the front of which in arched lettering was stenciled THE END, framing a grainy picture of the windswept clapboard establishment.

"Hey, Maggie, Maggie May."

"Hello, Bo," Maggie Meyers said before turning her attention to the bartender. She was a honey-gold babe with deep-set chestnut eyes and matching hair that she wore in a ponytail held by a rubber band.

After placing her order, Maggie said to Bo, "How's the tournament going?"

"We're in the finals." An uproar of laughter from the other end of the bar turned Bo's attention for a moment before he said to Maggie, "You're coming, right?"

She smiled yes.

It was a smile that had first caught Bo's eye last year, when he showed up at a kegger in a ramshackle house two blocks from the ocean that was rented by surfers. It was a loud, rambunctious bash, with the Doobie Brothers blasting out "Travelin' Man" on wall speakers. He spotted her in a corner standing by herself. She was wearing white cutoffs highlighting her shapely tan legs, and curves in all the right places gave shape to an untucked flannel shirt rolled to the sleeves. There was something wholesomely voluptuous about her, not just the body but her lovely face—more specifically her eyes, something mischievous, something knowing, as if she lived by her own set of rules and took life as it rolled by.

Bo walked over to her. "Hey there," he said, his chin tilted just so, smiling big, his light eyes glittering. "Beer and a doobie for the pretty girl?" He dug into his shorts pocket and revealed a fat joint.

She leaned forward, reading the writing in bold red letters on Bo's white T-shirt—He Who Dies with the Best Tan Wins.

"What about the living?" Her big brown eyes took in Bo in one swooping gaze, from his sun-bleached straw-blond hair to his bronze face and chiseled body, down his long legs to his T-strap sandals.

Bo studied her for a moment and then said, "I'm Bo." He lifted his chin as if to say, "Your turn."

"You didn't answer my question." She was looking at Bo as though searching for defects.

"I'm just a PE grad from UCLA who plays volleyball and makes a little money on the side." He lifted his brow—*your move*. Bo was enjoying this, though he knew he was in over his head.

She laughed lightly and said, "I'm Maggie, by the way."

Soon they were a couple, not a let's-get-married-someday couple but more two people living in the moment. Maggie was smart but rarely revealed it. And Bo was glad of it—not that he considered himself dumb. He did graduate college, after all, but he was never one to discuss politics or philosophical issues.

No, Bo liked to take each day as it came, whether it was getting a call to model beachwear for a local mail order company or playing volleyball either in a league or a tournament like today's, where more than half the bar left to attend the finals.

The sand court was set up on the back end of the beach, two players per team, separated by a seven-foot-high net. Mingled among the crowd were players who had played earlier and lost, still wearing their tank top jerseys, and the ever-present beach babes, some dressed in bikinis, others in short shorts and a halter top or a T-shirt.

During warm-ups, Bo saw Maggie making her way along the beach, as surfers came down off the face of a wave, cross-stepping agilely as they steered their boards toward shore. Maggie worked her way to the front row and threw a wave at Bo, who nodded back.

The match was best of three, and the teams split the first two. In the third set, Bo and his teammate, Cody, were gaining momentum with humongous spikes and great diving saves, all accompanied by ohs and ahs from the beach babes.

When Bo's team was within one point of victory, their opponents called a time-out. Bo stood on the sideline immersed in a strategic conversation with Cody, but at the same time there was a glancing awareness on his part of a nubile young woman watching his every move. Like Bo, she had light blue eyes and golden hair, and, if that wasn't enough, she had a bombshell body barely covered in a blood-red bikini.

This wasn't the first time Bo had drawn an admiring eye, and to his surprise it never seemed to bother Maggie. In fact, she acted as though it was kind of cool that her guy drew such attention in this beach town that benefited from ocean breezes that not only provided clean, invigorating air but kept the temperature ten to twenty degrees cooler than the inland regions of Southern California—or SoCal, as some of the regulars at the bar called it.

Maggie was the first girl Bo had dated who wasn't in awe of him, wasn't in love with him. She enjoyed his company and the parties and the life in this land of benevolent sun, but she was her own person. This bothered Bo and drew him to her like no girl he had ever been with. He kept this to himself, though it wouldn't surprise him if Maggie knew. He figured he was one kill shot away from getting dumped for the first time in his life.

Bo's team won match point, with Bo making a diving save that Cody spiked in the corner for the win. After the winners had received their trophies, the mingling of beautiful bodies came together with a no-strings-attached casualness that Maggie had told Bo was "so Southern California."

Bo was surrounded by other players and the beach babes, taking it all in with a sideways glance at Maggie—*Isn't this great?* Bo was in his wheelhouse, fun in the sun with all the extras that came with being a stud volleyballer. Maggie had told him he was the quintessential California beach boy. He took it as a compliment.

As the crowd began to thin out, the bikini girls returning to their blankets to bask under the late-afternoon sun, the players remained, talking in their baller lingo about the games played. "Killer sprawl, Bo." "Cody, great spike, dude." It was a movie Bo never tired of, but lately Maggie had a *been there, done that* look in her eyes, and not just at volleyball matches.

After seemingly every play of the tournament had been hashed over by Bo and company, he approached Maggie. "Guard party in the Hill Section." Bo made a face—*What do you think?*

The hill section was Maggie's neighborhood and where most of the parties were, and all had a similar theme—cornucopia of marijuana, keg of beer, and loud music. The only difference was the locations, which rotated from rental houses occupied by surfers, lifeguards, and volleyballers. They were a party-hearty lot that abused their bodies at night and replenished them during the day under the ever-present California sunshine.

"I have to finish my shift at the End," Maggie said. "Meet you there after I get off?"

CHAPTER 2

After the last customer had left and all the tables were cleared and cleaned, Nora Crowder sat at the bar and counted out her tips. It had been a busy and profitable Saturday-night shift, waiting tables in the back room where the younger crowd hung out.

Nora had been working at McDonald's Raw Bar, a family-run operation in the heart of downtown Bethesda for nearly two years, and besides the good money she made in tips, she knew most of the clientele. Many of the customers she had gone to school with either in grade school or high school at Walter Johnson.

A couple of months after getting hired at the Raw Bar, Nora had secured a two-bedroom apartment at Parkside, an older community surrounded by parkland that was just a ten-minute ride from work.

As luck would have it, a friend of a friend was looking for a place. Alicia worked for the federal government, and her only caveat was that if transferred, she was only obligated to pay one month's rent. Fair enough.

The caveat became a reality a few months after Nora had renewed the lease for a year.

But, in a way, Nora was relieved, since she and Alicia lived in two different worlds. Alicia was often away on business trips, and when home she would keep to herself in her room. It was like living with a ghost.

Nora couldn't afford the rent by herself, or maybe she could, but she didn't want to live alone. Not just the security issue, but Nora wanted someone to talk with, to be friends with.

Back at her apartment at half past midnight, Nora noticed Alicia's bedroom door was ajar, signaling she was not home.

Nora unlocked the balcony door and slid it open. It was late October, the air brisk but not yet unbearable. The wind rustled through the trees that appeared like a black amorphous wall. The moon peeked out from behind a cloud, illuminating the forest in a pale yellow light.

She took the moon's appearance as a sign, to play a hunch she had been considering. She decided to call an old high school friend, who had moved cross country from Bethesda to Northern California to attend a small liberal arts college nine years ago. After graduating, she had worked her way down the coast until landing a waitressing job in Manhassa Beach a couple of years back. "I tired of the nine-to-five grind and decided to enjoy life," Maggie Meyers had told Nora.

Nora still liked to think of Maggie as her best friend even though they only talked on the phone a couple of times a year. They had hung out at Hot Shoppes together every Friday night all through the high school years at WJ, double-dated, and attended parties together, just the two of them.

Maggie had told Nora something she never forgot. "Don't let a guy think he is the be all and end all—keep him guessing." And Maggie always held true to that belief, never falling head over heels for any boy. Nora used to call her the Heartbreak Kid.

"Nora," Maggie said with a lift in her voice.

It always felt great to hear Maggie's voice, always confident and assured as if she was on top of things.

After an exchange of greetings, Maggie asked if Nora was still at the Raw Bar.

"Yes, and it has a younger crowd these days, kids we went to school with who went there with their parents."

Nora asked about life on the West Coast.

"It's good," Maggie said in an unconvincing tone, a tone Nora didn't recall hearing before.

"Still dating the volleyball guy?"

"Yeah," Maggie said, "studly *dud*, Bo."

"Same old same old?"

"I've had my fill of volleyball." Maggie cleared her throat as if to change the subject. "How are things going back in B-town?"

"My roommate is moving out. She received a transfer to Kansas City."

"Really," Maggie said in a tone that said, *Tell me more.*

"Parkside Apartments," Nora said.

"I remember you telling me, garden apartments right next to Rock Creek Park."

"Uh huh," Nora said. "Are you thinking of coming back to Bethesda?"

"Well—"

"Opening at the Raw Bar ..."

CHAPTER 3

When Maggie didn't show for the party at the guard house, Bo decided to walk the four blocks to her apartment. It was one in the morning, and the town was quiet other than the crashing roar of the ocean, which if the wind was right could be heard all over town. The shimmering moonlight reflecting off the water and the invigorating sea-salty air reminded Bo why he loved living in Manhassa Beach.

Maggie lived by herself in one of three units in a board-and-batten beach bungalow, two blocks up from the ocean. He tapped on the front door and waited. Tapped again and when he got no answer, he walked around to Maggie's bedroom window, which was raised. Bo peeked in through the screen and saw Maggie asleep under the covers, her head facing toward him.

Part of Bo didn't like coming over like this, so un-Bo-like. The other, stronger, part could not help it. She was like an addiction. What was it? He had dated girls just as good-looking, even some with better bodies. But it was her spirit, something about her that he couldn't put his finger on that made her so damn hard to resist. "Psst, Maggie. Maggie."

Maggie stirred but didn't wake.

"Maggie," Bo said in a raised voice.

Maggie's eyes opened, and she stared at Bo for a moment. She wasn't happy. Then she made a face as if to say, "Might as well get it over with."

Bo knew what was coming.

Maggie got up and told Bo to go around to the front door.

At the door, Bo asked her if they could take a walk.

Maggie, dressed in a gray sleeping gown, gazed at Bo with sleep-flecked eyes. But behind the sleepy gaze there was a trace of compassion like a sympathetic executioner about to lower the guillotine. She raised a finger to indicate *just a minute.*

She returned wearing jeans and her The End T-shirt.

They walked silently down the street toward the ocean, until Maggie said, "I've decided to head back east."

"What?" Bo said as they stopped. He looked up the street, crammed with beach bungalows of various shapes and colors. Not only was she breaking up, but leaving for the East Coast. Bo felt a strong sense of resentment at not only Maggie's dumping him but her leaving his beloved SoCal.

"Can't explain it," Maggie said, "but, I need to go back to Bethesda for a while." She shrugged as if to indicate that it was out of her hands.

Bo flicked a wayward lank of hair off his forehead and made a face. "Bethesda?"

"Time to move on, Bo," Maggie said.

Bo turned to the sound of a mellow-yellow jeep, with the top down, rumbling up the street. The jeep stopped. It was Cody and another volleyballer.

"Bo, my man," Cody hooted. "All-night kegger at Surfer Dude's." It was the house at which Bo and Maggie had first met.

Bo smirked a look at Maggie and offered her a half salute. "Later," he said. He then got in the tight storage area behind the two front seats, sitting across the width of the vehicle, his back to Maggie, and off they went, Bo never looking back.

CHAPTER 4

M aggie found Bethesda much the same, a middle-class town of friendly folks, with a blue-collar element attracted to anything automotive. Bordering Northwest DC, the communities were mostly built in the '50s and '60s, time enough to provide foliage, and especially at Parkside Apartments, which was surrounded by parkland. Being back and rooming with Nora was great—spades on a lazy afternoon, bingo at the Knights, sharing a meal at the apartment, and reminiscing and laughing about high school.

But toward the end of Maggie's second week in Bethesda, she was beginning to have second thoughts about leaving Manhassa Beach.

Parkside was much quieter than Manhassa Beach, which at first seemed a good thing, but Maggie missed the beachy lifestyle that she had thought she'd grown tired of—the shouts of partiers in the alleyways at all hours, the hum of energy at the Endless Summer, and the easy-as-you-please living. Bethesda seemed surburbanly slow and stifling and not with it in comparison. Whatever had she been thinking to return home?

It wasn't as though she were miserable living and working in Bethesda. Waiting tables at McDonald's Raw Bar was an enjoyable, good-paying job. Maggie was making more money than at the End.

The Raw Bar was located on Old Georgetown Road, situated in a row of small businesses. The outside had a brick façade and triangular-shaped awning over the wooden front door with a porthole window. The interior was divided into three flowing spaces—the front room with tables and booths; in the middle was the bar where the old-timers hung out; and the back room, which had light pine paneling, scuffed linoleum floors, and a ship-wheel's clock on the wall providing a nautical flair. It was a worn, comfortable place where everybody knew your name.

It wasn't the Raw Bar or really even Bethesda, where Maggie had nothing but good memories of growing up in, but more the constant current of vitality of Manhassa Beach—falling asleep and then waking up to the salty sounds and scents of living by the Pacific Ocean, being able to walk to and from work, and then those damn parties that she thought she had tired of, with the unique smell of marijuana mingling with salt air and beer.

But she had committed to the remaining eight months on the lease with Nora and would see it through and go from there. She told herself she was on a sabbatical from the West Coast, and when she returned, she would appreciate it all the more.

And then it all changed—everything. It was Maggie's first Friday night at the Raw Bar, and she was working the back room. Nora, who had the evening off, had told Maggie ahead of time that "The round table is reserved every Friday for a group of guys who play basketball at Bethesda Elementary."

They were mostly big shoulders and all with that athletic swagger to them, and as they sat at the round table, in the middle of the space, Maggie was stunned for a moment. There *he* was among this collection of large bodies. He was older, thirty by her quick calculation, but Johnny O'Brien still looked very much the same, a young-adult version of himself as a teenager. Maggie gathered herself and came over to the table to take their orders. "So this must be the boys from Bethesda I've heard so much about."

"That'd be us," Johnny said as their eyes met. Something clicked. Something that swept her back to that first time she had seen him—something.

Three grades ahead of Maggie, Johnny O'Brien had been a star athlete at Walter Johnson, where Maggie's dad had volunteered as an assistant coach to the football team. Ninth-grader Maggie attended every one of the games, home and away. Johnny was the quarterback and moved like lightning in a bottle.

And she would never forget the first time she saw his face when he removed his helmet at the end of the season opener at WJ, which Johnny had won with a weaving, impossible run in the last seconds. It wasn't just the thicket of wavy dark hair, or the perfectly formed features with the cheekbones set high and wide, but later, as the team made its way up the stands to the locker room, *click-clacking* of cleats on the concrete steps, he passed right by Maggie, and she was thunderstruck by the dark blue eyes that transmitted a gracious confidence. And, of course, there was something in his countenance, a certain, yet unassuming, aura that correlated with an electric presence, which had seemed to influence not only his teammates during the game, but the entire stands as he stopped to accept congratulations from parents and students. No one could take their eyes off of Johnny O'Brien.

Maggie had fallen head over heels for a boy she had never met. He was her own private heartthrob. After that season, she never laid eyes on him again until this very moment.

One of the guys at the table asked Maggie her name. "Maggie," she replied. "What's yours, Slim?"

This cracked up the table. "Hah, hah, Slim," the biggest one in the group said. "You're okay, honey." He then began introducing each of the boys until, "This is Johnny."

"Hello, Johnny," Maggie said, trying her damndest to maintain her poise. "You look like a cold-beer kinda guy."

Johnny nodded, his eyes taking in this new girl before him. "Looks like you got me figured out, Maggie." He smiled easy, his eyes still on her.

After Maggie took their order, she tended to her other customers. But she kept her eyes and ears on these boys from Bethesda, who were a hooting and hollering gregarious bunch, playing liars poker, discussing the pickup b-ball games, and needling each other in that friendly malicious boys-will-be-boys way. All the while, Maggie exchanged an occasional glance at Johnny, who was taking it all in, interjecting a bon mot from time to time. He was even more handsome than she had remembered and, as she discovered, entertaining.

After the Friday-night basketball crew had eaten and ordered another round of beers, Brad, the big guy, said to Johnny, "Time to let Scruffy Lomax out of the box."

Maggie placed two frothy pitchers in the middle of the table and said to Johnny, "I'd love to meet Scruffy." She wasn't sure what this was all about but sure did want to find out.

Then Brad began pounding the table with his fist. "We want Scruffy ... We want Scruffy ..." and then the rest of the table, followed by the entire back room, began the chant.

Johnny raised his hand over his head and stood at the table. The room fell into a murmuring silence. Johnny lowered his head as though praying. "Scruffy, you in there? ... I'm here, pardner," Johnny said out of the side of his mouth with an earthy twang like an old-timer in a '50s western. "Let me out to say hi to the good folks at the Raw Bar." Johnny looked around the table, his buddies all smiling big with anticipation, as were the rest in the room. "You promise to behave?" Johnny said in his regular voice.

"'Promise,'" Scruffy growled.

"All righty, then." Johnny slid a quick look at Maggie, his eyes grinning as if to say, "Are you with me?"

Indeed I am, Maggie thought.

Johnny then squeezed his shoulders in, drew his chin into his neck, and said in his gravelly Scruffy voice, "Pardners, so good to be back in your company. Ha-ha-ha."

A young woman sitting at a corner table with her date said, "Story time, Scruffy."

Maggie looked around the room, and all eyes were on Johnny. It reminded her of the high school football game when Johnny was walking up the steps, everyone looking upon the young star.

"Well, since I last saw you folks," Johnny said in his Scruffy rasp, "me and Rusty the one-eyed wonder dog and Needle Nose Latrobe were up in Yukon Territory prospecting when we run into Hilty the man-eating grizzly—biggest damn bear you ever did see." Johnny paused and looked around the room with the squinty-eyed look of an old-timer telling a bedtime story to kiddies. "Then a hellacious blizzard hit, snow blowing sideways, and we didn't know to be more worried about the storm or the griz."

Johnny was in character. He was Scruffy Lomax. Maggie could not take her eyes off of him, her mind transported back to ninth grade, the girl with the huge crush on a boy she had never met.

And it was not just Maggie; the entire room was drawn to Johnny's charm. The young woman and her date were listening with rapt attention as though believing every word.

"Well, first off, Rusty gives that big old bear the evil eye." Johnny shut one eye while the other seemed to launch from its socket. He did a 360 around the room, giving everyone a good look. "And Hilty, the big bad bear, let out a shriek and hightailed it into the teeth of that storm." Johnny offered a bemused Scruffy smile, the eyes crinkled into two slits, the mouth a thin smirk. "And then the real challenge began …"

Scruffy went on to tell a harrowing tale of two men and a little dog fighting the elements until all three made it safely back to Big Bear, Alaska. Johnny, still in character, raised a finger as if to indicate one more thing. "We entered the Lone Branch chilled to the bone, with Rusty tucked in the crook of me arm, bellied up to the bar, ordered drinks on the house, and with raised shot of Irish whiskey, I proclaimed, 'Once again I have beaten death and live to fight another day.'"

Johnny received a loud round of applause from the room. He bowed and then sat and took a sip of his beer. He then raised his brow in Maggie's direction, a sheepish smile. He shrugged and said, "Maggie, what did you think of Scruffy?"

She was standing at the waitress station, one table over. "Love Scruffy," she said with a confirming nod. *And if you give me a chance, you too, Johnny O'Brien,* Maggie said to herself.

By last call, Johnny and one of the boys, Danny, were all who remained in the back room. The check had been paid, and they sat with a half-full pitcher of beer. Maggie had finished wiping down the tables, and Johnny asked her to join them.

She came over with an empty mug, poured herself a beer, and raised it to Johnny. "Ever had a chilly?"

"Like you said, I'm a cold-beer kinda guy." Johnny clinked her glass.

Danny began to raise his, but seemed to realize they barely even knew he was there.

"Tell me about yourself, Maggie," Johnny said.

"Left B-town for college in California and have lived there ever since," she said.

"You sticking around?" Johnny asked

Maggie shrugged and took a drink of beer. She shrugged again and said, "Depends."

Danny soon departed, and it was just the two of them. They chatted amiably about nothing of consequence for a while, and then Johnny reached over and placed his hand on top of hers. "You're different."

Maggie flashed a smile at Johnny. "Your hand is like rawhide." She took his hand in hers and ran her fingers in a circle on his palm.

"Work."

"Ah," Maggie said as she stared at Johnny's palm. "Let me guess, carpenter."

"Landscaper."

Maggie continued to study Johnny's hand and then traced her index finger along a horizontal line. "You have a fate line." She looked up at Johnny. "They're rare." She ran her finger along the line until it intersected a horizontal line toward the top of his hand. "It intersects your heart line."

"They're intertwined," Johnny said in a factual tone. He seemed to catch himself and said, "Are you a palm reader?"

"No," Maggie said. She looked at Johnny and saw a look of confident interest. "My great-aunt had some gypsy blood." She crinkled her eyes in self-depreciating delight. "We all have our secrets."

Johnny laced his fingers through hers and said, "You really are different, aren't you?"

The Sunday after they had met at the Raw Bar, Johnny took Maggie to a late-afternoon movie and then dinner at an Italian restaurant across the line into DC. The place had an old-world charm, with a stone fireplace, checkered tablecloths, and grainy photos on the wall of unsmiling relatives, the men uncomfortable-looking in suits, the women in long dresses and aprons.

"Booth or table?" Johnny said to Maggie as a man in a dark suit approached. He was heavyset with dark, thinning hair, and he greeted them with a warm, if insincere, smile. "Welcome," he said drawing the word out in a singsongy Italian accent, *welllcooome*. Maggie figured him to be the owner.

"Good evening," Johnny said as he looked over the nearly empty space, a few people at a bar in the back, the booths on both sides empty, and a few tables in the middle with diners. "May we sit …" Johnny said glancing at Maggie.

"Booth, on the left in the middle," Maggie said to Johnny.

"We would like a booth," Johnny said as he extended his arm, finger pointing to the chosen location. "That one."

The proprietor offered a courtly tilt of his head. "Of course," he said as he swept a hand off to his side.

The waiter, dressed in a white shirt, bow tie, and black vest came over. Johnny said to Maggie, "Cold chilly?"

Maggie smiled yes and said, "Let's split a pitcher."

After Johnny ordered, he said, "I knew you were a girl from Bethesda when you asked if I'd ever had a chilly."

"People out west don't have a clue what it means."

"It's a Bethesda thing," Johnny said.

"First time I heard it was at a deserted, dead-end street out in Potomac—"

"Tara Road," Johnny said as he looked up at the *whoosh* of the front door opening. "Schlitz," Johnny hooted in a rallying cry, hands raised over head.

Maggie turned and saw someone she hadn't seen since high school, Mark "Schlitz" O'Halloran, a legendary party animal. And he still looked the part—heavily built like a Buick Roadmaster, though he carried it well with big shoulders, thick torso, a respectable beer belly, and the map of Ireland across his broad, freckled face, a face that still had a look that said, "It's party time."

"Oh my God," Schlitz said as he came up to the table and saw Maggie and Johnny together. Maggie got up and hugged Schlitz.

Schlitz smiled big at the couple before him, the eyes grinning like a kid in a candy store. He looked at Johnny, then back at Maggie, and nodded as if he approved. "We have worlds colliding."

"Sit down, Schlitz, you old rally king, you," Johnny said as Maggie slid in next to him and Schlitz sat across. "We were just discovering that we both had attended Happy Hour at Tara Road."

And so it began over two pitchers, reminisces about high school days. It turned out that Schlitz, who went to Walt Whitman High, and was a year behind Johnny and two ahead of Maggie, had known both during high school.

"Do you remember the time at Tara Road," Johnny said with a remembering look of utter joy, "when Dave Hodge put the flashing light on top—"

Schlitz cut in, "That was my light and my idea, Hodge's car." He smiled a shit-eating grin and said, "I saw you jump into the back of Kenny Bonner's Caddie convertible, Larry River riding shotgun, plowing through the woods, dirt and Mother Nature's debris a flying."

Johnny firmly shook his head at the memory. "I should have known who was behind it." Johnny looked at Maggie. "Those were the days." There was a look so innocent and yet appealing in Johnny's eyes. And in the company of Schlitz, it was magnified as though a light switch had been turned on.

Schlitz and Johnny mentioned names from the past, some Maggie knew and some not.

"Remember when the Dill brothers arrived at Shoppes looking to settle a score?" Schlitz said to Johnny.

"Chris and John, yeah," Johnny said with a nod. "Some guys from the Lourdes had roughed up a buddy of theirs. Found out they were at a party and went there and cleaned house."

Schlitz smiled big. "They were the *original* St. John's badasses."

Maggie was enjoying listening and adding a tidbit now and then. "Tara Road was like an open air bar with no adults. I almost felt like an urban outlaw."

Johnny put his arm around Maggie's shoulder and said, "Gotta love this girl, Schlitz."

In that moment of Johnny's embrace, Maggie felt a surge of comforting bliss; it felt so very right, before he and Schlitz were off again reminiscing.

"Remember the time at Hot Shoppes when Dude Newman and Corky Espinoza challenged those hot-rodding rednecks from Rockville to a rumble at the WJ football field?" Schlitz asked as he refilled all three glasses. "Larry Rivers told me if it wasn't for your quick thinking someone might have died that night."

Johnny tried to shrug it off, but Maggie said, "How's that, Schlitz?"

"Johnny and Danny McKenzie, I think it was ..." Schlitz looked at Johnny, who nodded yes. "They ran lickety-split to the cop station and warned about a big fight about to happen at WJ."

"Johnny O'Brien to the rescue," Maggie said as she slipped her arm through his and leaned into him.

Johnny took Maggie's hand in his and squeezed. Popping into her head was one of her all-time favorite songs, "This Magic Moment."

Johnny shrugged as if to say no biggie, and then wagged a finger at Schlitz. "Larry Rivers, now there was another party animal."

"Don't forget Kenny Bonner," Schlitz said.

"You three together," Johnny said as he laced his fingers through Maggie's, their hands resting on their thighs tight against each other, "were The Three Musketeers of Party at Whitman."

Maggie felt as though she were engaged in two conversations, one vocal and the other a silent, developing intimacy of hand-holding and sitting close together, both of which she was thoroughly enjoying. "Your honor, if I may make a correction for the record." Maggie raised her brow to Schlitz and then looked at Johnny with false seriousness. "They were the Three Musketeers of Tara Road."

"Correction duly noted," Johnny said. "And may I add to the record, their glorious rallying cry—"

Schlitz cut in in an uproarious voice. "Party hearty, Tara Road! Party hearty, Tara Road!'"

And so it went with Johnny and Schlitz reveling in "the good old days."

After the second pitcher was empty, Schlitz got up and waved to someone at the bar. "Got to go."

"One more pitcher, Schlitz," Johnny said.

"Two things," Schlitz said placing both hands on the table, "no make that three. First the beer is on me." He raised a hand to a protesting Johnny. "Heck, I drank most of it. I didn't get the name Schlitz for nothing." He leaned back, a bemused smile flickering around the corner of his mouth. "Second, I have to collect from my bookie. Redskins finally came through for me, *and …*" Schlitz said with an empathic tap of fingers on the table, "you two look great together." He shook his head and said through his big Irish grin, "Worlds colliding."

Maggie gave Schlitz a goodbye hug and then took his seat. Johnny sat across from her in silence, as though trying to bring himself back to the present time. His eyes brightened holding hers. "Let's chitchat a bit before we order."

"Chitchat it is," she said as she raised her glass and clinked Johnny's. "Bet you didn't know that I knew about you through my father."

"What?"

"He was an assistant coach on the WJ football team."

"Big Pat Meyers, who coached the line?" Johnny said as he looked away for a moment at the sound of a breaking glass.

"Yup."

"Great guy," Johnny said as they both glanced over at their waiter sweeping up a shattered mug into a dust bin. "How is the big man?"

"He died," Maggie said. "Heart attack my second year of college." Maggie felt a tug of sadness invade this perfect date.

"So sorry; what a great guy." Johnny looked off for a moment as though considering and then said, "We got something in common. I lost my father when I was ten." He looked at Maggie, and in his gaze she saw something beyond the loss of a father, something. He took a swallow of his beer, finishing it, and looked back at Maggie.

"Well, at least we have our mothers," Johnny said.

"No," Maggie said, wishing they weren't going down this path, but she might as well get it all out. "My mother died two years after my father, breast cancer."

Johnny reached across the table and took Maggie's hand in his. He told her how sorry he was and asked about any siblings.

"None," Maggie said. "Only child."

"Me too."

They exchanged looks, the silent code of intimacy between them, before Maggie said, "I went to every one of your football games your senior year, home and away."

She made a face—*how about that.* She wanted to tell him that she'd had a crush on him the first time she saw him after that first game but held back.

All through high school, she thought about where he was and what he was doing. Later not so much, but still from time to time that indelible moment she saw him up close would surface from the back recesses of her mind.

Johnny went on to tell Maggie about growing up, "Right next to Ayrlawn Rec Center. Me and my friends were down there all summer and every day after school."

Maggie said she had been raised in Ashburton, a Bethesda community, less than a mile north of Johnny's house.

"Some of the kids at Ayrlawn called it Trashburton," Johnny said with a laugh.

"I heard that," Maggie said with mock ire as the waiter came over, and they ordered dinner and another pitcher of beer.

They talked through the meal, and after, Johnny asked the waiter for a napkin and if he could borrow a pen. "Just sit there and be you," Johnny told Maggie as he shielded the napkin with one hand, while he would draw and then look up at her, his hand and eyes working in unison.

When he had finished, he removed his hand and turned it over for Maggie to see. It was so good, not only the similarity to her face, but it captured the essence of who Maggie was. It was the eyes, her eyes that even in this sketch on a napkin radiated a wondering keen, a searching.

On the bottom, Johnny had written in perfect Old English fonts, "The girl who takes the road less traveled."

"I love it, and the poem it was taken from," Maggie said. "May I keep it?"

"Something to remember me by," Johnny said in a faraway voice, before catching himself and offering a shrug and a tight smile.

There was something weighing on Johnny, the momentary gritty slant to the eyes, the pursed lips, a dark cloud draping his countenance. "Johnny," Maggie said, reaching across the table for his hand, "you can tell me anything."

At Maggie's front door, Johnny leaned forward and kissed her on the lips. Before she could ask him in, Johnny said in a soft, singsongy voice, "'I'd like to get to know you, yes, I would.'" He kissed her again, stepped back, and crossed his arm over his waist and bowed. "Good night, fair maiden."

As Maggie closed the door, California seemed to drift away as though it had broken off from the continent and swallowed up by the ocean.

CHAPTER 5

B efore Johnny, Maggie Meyers had never been one for sticking out a relationship. Once she had experienced all the layers of a guy, she moved on—been there, done that. Life was too short. See you later, Bo Ricker.

But Johnny O'Brien was different. Maggie had met, at the very least, her equal. He had everything she had—good looks, smarts, and charisma oozing out of every pore of his handsome being. And then there was his chivalrous side that revealed itself the first night they went out. She would have let him in her apartment and shared her bed with him, but he offered her only a kiss good night and a song. And in his eyes that first night was a look that said, "We have time, and when we get to know each other, it will be wonderful." Johnny O'Brien was all ninth-grader Maggie Meyers had ever imagined and then some.

Their second date was at the Brickskeller in Georgetown, a tavern in the basement of a hotel, which had a rustic saloon motif with beer memorabilia adorning the aged brick walls. The place was crowded, and they shared a table with another couple, not what Maggie was hoping for.

But after introductions were made, some small talk about the choice of beers, and orders were placed, Johnny turned his attention to Maggie. He looked at her as though she was the only person in the room. "Has anyone ever told you, Maggie Meyers, that you are a beautiful woman, not just on the outside, but in here," Johnny said, placing his hand over his heart.

It wasn't just the words that were said, but the expression on Johnny's face of someone discovering a great find for the first time in his life.

From that moment, the evening sailed on, Johnny inquiring and commenting on life in California. "I would love to try surfing and beach volleyball. It all sounds like a blast."

Maggie thought how seamlessly Johnny would have fit in at Manhassa Beach, the East Coast guy who was not only a very fine athlete, but with a quick wit and inquisitive brain, something rare among the beach hunks. Maggie could see a beach babe saying to him, "Oooo, you're different." Maggie would have wanted to scratch her eyes out for even looking at Johnny. Unlike Bo, this fellow was a keeper.

But Maggie wondered if Johnny would have tired of the life of sun and fun, maybe quicker, much quicker, than she had.

Later that night, when they returned to Maggie's apartment, she thought about asking Johnny in but decided to let him play it out. At the front door, Johnny said, "I'll say yes, if you invite me inside."

Maggie turned to unlock the door and said over her shoulder, "I was hoping you would ask."

They made love for the first time that night, the likes of which Maggie had never experienced. It wasn't just his beautifully proportioned body, lean and firm with everything seemingly in perfect symmetry, but the rhythmic passion of the act itself. It was as if they were one entity sharing two bodies.

Afterward, as he held her in his arms, they lay naked in bed face to face, no words spoken, no words needed. It was at that moment, that very moment, that Maggie knew she would risk anything to spend the rest of her life with Johnny O'Brien.

CHAPTER 6

Maggie was in love, real love, for the first time. It was so intense that she sometimes felt an ache in her chest when she hadn't seen Johnny for a while, especially now, during springtime with his landscaping business. Johnny was a one-man operation, "Simpler that way," he had told her. He had the ability to expand the business. Johnny was very smart and personable, but growing his one-man operation did not interest him. The future did not seem to interest him. "I take it a day at a time," he had told Maggie.

Johnny's two best friends, Danny McKenzie and Tip Durham, would sometimes stop by the Raw Bar on Saturday afternoons, Johnny still at work. It was a quiet time, and Maggie had an opportunity to sit down and talk with them. Danny was a CPA, and Tip worked in the swimming pool business. Like Johnny, Danny and Tip were single; the remainder of the Friday-night basketball crowd were married.

Danny and Tip would regale Maggie with stories about growing up at Ayrlawn. "Time of our lives," Danny said. They were sitting at a corner table in the back room.

"I think if his mother would have let him," Tip said with a wink and a nod, "Johnny would have slept at Ayrlawn in the summer and only come home for meals."

Tip and Danny exchanged glances, and their eyes let it be known that they too might have slept there during the summer.

"How about the legendary quarter-flipping episode with Mike Andros first day of junior high at North Bethesda?" Danny asked.

"Cockiest kid I ever saw," Tip said.

"Smart too," Danny added. "Smart as Johnny."

"Yeah, well," Tip said, "Johnny cleaned him out flipping quarters, and I loved it."

The two never tired of telling Maggie stories about Johnny, and she never tired of listening. "He really has it all, Maggie," Danny said. "He could be or do anything in this life he wanted, but he has no interest to grow his business."

That something about Johnny, Danny had also noticed. "Ever since fifth grade when his father died, sometimes he will go off inside himself," Danny said.

"Yes," Maggie said, "it's like he's holding something back. Something he wants to tell me but can't—or won't—let it out."

"Whatever it is, it seems to hold him back in life," Danny said. "Tip and I wanted him to get an apartment with us." Danny shook his head at the memory.

"No way," Tip piped in. "He will never leave his mother."

"Yeah," Danny said as leaned forward in his chair, hands folded on the table. "His mom never recovered from the death of his dad. They are very close. Says it would kill her if he moved out."

"I've been invited to dinner at his mother's house tomorrow," Maggie said.

"That's a first," Danny said.

Maggie drove herself over to Mary O'Brien's home, a little white box nestled under a weeping willow tree. The neat and orderly exterior fit Johnny, nothing fancy, other than the immaculate dark green lawn and neatly spaced flower beds along the front of the house. The siding looked freshly painted, as did the light gray shutters.

Johnny greeted Maggie at the front door, and immediately she smelled a confluence of aromas—bread baking in the oven, garlicky tomato meat sauce with a hint of something else that she couldn't put her finger on.

Maggie stepped into the foyer, and Johnny gave her a peck on the cheek. "Smells wonderful in here, Johnny," Maggie said as he ushered her into the living room. Much like the exterior, the interior was no muss, no fuss with a living room/dining room space, which was separated only by the variation in furnishings. The floor was covered by beige wall-to-wall carpeting.

In the doorless kitchen, off to the left, Mary O'Brien was wearing a smock apron with tiny red polka dots over her white buttoned-down blouse and gray skirt. She had a filter-tipped cigarette between her ring and middle finger, while in the other hand a wooden spatula stirred the contents of a cast iron pot on the stove.

Johnny's mother looked over her shoulder. "Hello there," she said in a monotone voice, not unfriendly but not welcoming either.

Mary O'Brien was a full-figured woman with wavy, raven-black hair cut above the shoulder in a soft tumble of curls, her eyes dark blue, like Johnny's, but without the sunshine, and her skin ivory white. She appeared to be one of those strong-willed Black Irish women who were set in their ways.

Maggie said hello back, standing there next to Johnny in the foyer, waiting for the next move in this social dance.

"Johnny, you two," Mary said with a regal wave of her hand toward the living room, "make yourselves at home, and I will join you shortly."

"All righty," Johnny said as he moved toward the kitchen, "how about I make you an Old Fashioned and grab a couple of beers for me and Maggie."

"Hmmm," Mary said drawing her chin into her neck, brow raised. "You drink beer?" she said to Maggie.

"Mom." Johnny laughed and put his arm around his mother's shoulder and gave her a squeeze. "Get with the times." He laughed again, threw a smile at Maggie, and told her to have a seat.

And so the evening went, mother and son and their guest sitting in the living room, making idle conversation, while the dinner simmered on the stove: Johnny and Maggie drinking a beer—Maggie asked for a glass—and Mary O'Brien her Old Fashioned, which she sipped on, while holding a cigarette with cocked elbow set on the armrest. All the while, Mary was smiling on cue when needed, but never diverting the focus of her attention away from her son, other than a glance here and there in Maggie's direction, while Johnny appeared oblivious to it all.

Johnny finished his beer and asked Maggie if she would like another.

Mary aimed a sharp-eyed look directed at Maggie, who was beginning to feel like a trespasser in Mother O'Brien's private domain.

Maggie had been careful in slowly drinking her beer. "No thanks, Johnny," she said through a polite smile, though part of her was tempted to chug-a-lug her remaining beer down and shout, "Love one!"

Mrs. O'Brien asked Johnny to check the pot on the stove and with a sideways look toward Maggie said, "I do hope you like spaghetti and meatballs." She flashed a smile over her shoulder at her son, stirring the spaghetti. "It's Johnny's favorite."

Johnny returned to his seat, popped open his beer, and said, "My mom's a great cook."

Mother and son exchanged another smile, and Maggie was struck by the looks of mutual admiration.

Maggie said that she liked all Italian food and then with a lift of her chin toward the kitchen said, "There is one ingredient my nostrils can't identify."

Mary smiled her patented smile. "Oh, that's my secret ingredient, fresh basil that Johnny and I grow in the garden in the backyard."

Another mutual exchange of smiles between mother and son. They reminded Maggie of members of a secret club.

The conversation during the meal revolved around Mary and Johnny discussing all things Catholic: the Knights of Columbus, of which Johnny was a member; Mary mentioning, "The new young priest at Lourdes has some radical ideas, which ..." she waved a hand as though to dismiss the subject, "I can't even talk about," and Catholic charities where Mary did volunteer work.

Maggie was praying that Mary didn't ask her about her religious affiliation. She was raised Catholic but had quit attending services as soon as she went to college. But she needn't have worried, for Mary showed little interest in her guest during cocktail hour and then during the meal, and to top it off, she never addressed Maggie by her name.

After they had finished eating, Johnny stood from the dinner table and said, "Mom, you relax, and I'll clear the table and do the dishes."

"No, honey," Mary said with half-conviction.

"Moommm," Johnny said, drawing the word out. He widened his eyes and said, "No arguments. Now you and Maggie get acquainted."

"Very well," Mary said as she offered a hand toward the living room.

Maggie returned to the sofa where she and Johnny had previously sat, and Mary returned to her high-back chair. All she needed was a crown atop her head.

And, *getting acquainted* was met with an awkward silence before Maggie said, "Wonderful dinner, Mrs. O'Brien."

Maggie received a nod of the head—the queen acknowledging her subject—and a curt "thank you."

Mrs. O'Brien rearranged herself in her chair, glanced over her shoulder at Johnny scrubbing away in the kitchen, and folded her hands on her lap. She then honed in on Maggie sitting on the sofa and said in a nasally tone hinting ever so slightly of disapproval, "So, I hear you are a waitress."

At the end of the evening, Johnny walked Maggie out to her car. "My mom takes a little getting used to," he said as he opened her car door.

You think? Maggie thought, as she smiled and nodded.

On the way home, Maggie remembered the old saying about always meeting the family before marriage. Johnny understood his mother was difficult, but more as a quirky characteristic as opposed to a character flaw. As Maggie stopped for a red light at Rockville Pike, a nascent thought crept into her mind: Mary O'Brien could present a formidable obstacle in the courtship of Johnny O'Brien.

CHAPTER 7

Maggie ladled the last of the meatballs into a pot of spaghetti sauce. She wanted to impress Johnny with her own version of his favorite meal. Maggie had to throw it all together rather quickly since Johnny had asked yesterday on the phone if they could be alone instead of going to a party at Brad's house. Johnny rarely, if ever, missed an opportunity to be around his boys. Something was up. He then blurted out in a hurried voice. "There's something I would like to discuss with you, Maggie." *Something?* Maggie thought. *Could it be?*

They had been dating for six month, and Maggie wondered if he was finally going to ask her what she had been hoping for a while now: marriage and even having Johnny's baby. She had never considered any of this before and never remotely thought about having a child. But Johnny O'Brien had changed all of that. And she had even done something reckless, something she had always been careful about. Maggie had not taken her birth control pills for the last month. It was an intuitive maneuver, an instinctive sense that it was the right thing to do. Why that was, she did not know. But the sense of it was overpowering.

However this evening was to play out, Maggie would let the night unfold, or more correctly, let Johnny unfold the night as he saw fit.

Jumping the gun was not Maggie's normal path; it had always been the guy who wanted to shove the relationship forward. Deep down, Maggie had squashed below the surface a part of herself trying to alert her to be careful with Johnny. Not only the odd relationship with his stilted, stuffy mother, but also those moments where he went inside himself; Maggie thought of it as his Johnny deep-down-in-the-dumps face. But it never lasted long before he snapped back to his old self.

But Maggie did wonder what *that* was, for in that moment there was a look upon his face of utter desolation.

It was a Saturday night, and with Nora out of town, Maggie and Johnny would have the apartment to themselves. She greeted him at the door with a frosted mug of beer. "Ever had a chilly?" she said through her most beguiling of smiles.

Johnny hung up his jacket in the closet and took a deep whiff. "It smells great in here; reminds me of my mother's."

Maggie wasn't sure how to receive that comment, but she swept the thought from her mind as he kissed her on the cheek.

Johnny smiled and said, "Hello, stranger." They hadn't seen each other for the last week, Maggie just getting over the flu and, being springtime, Johnny busy with work.

They exchanged looks, and for a moment Maggie thought he was going to ask her right there. *Yes,* she wanted to scream to him. *Yes, Johnny O'Brien, I will marry you!* But then she saw a shadow of hesitant uncertainty before the confident cast returned.

Maggie hoped, oh, did she hope, that the hesitation was nothing, a temporary work-related problem in the inner workings of this multitalented young man. A man who could make up a witty and humorous story, with all the effects of an old raconteur; a man who could draw landscape blueprints lickety-split or a portrait on a napkin as he did of Maggie on their first date; a man of effortless charm that seemingly no one was immune to. Formidable mother notwithstanding, she would marry him.

They sat in the living room on a squishy sofa, Maggie with a glass of red wine, Johnny his beer. Johnny always liked to take in the room, having told Maggie how much he liked the decor. The space had offset shelves of odds and ends: a cottage clock, miniature lantern, and a metal vase with daisies, most of it Nora's. His gaze drifted over to the corner to a three-tier wire storage stand, each shelf containing a bird's nest with a colorful songbird nesting.

Maggie asked how work was coming.

Johnny looked out the sliding glass door at the wet, blustery weather.

He shrugged nonchalantly and said he was behind schedule. Johnny turned to Maggie and offered his beautiful smile.

She hoped this was where the proposal would come. But then a glint sparked in his eyes, a glint she knew by now. She needed to stay calm and relaxed and remember to let Johnny do it his way.

"How is the patient feeling?" Johnny said.

Maggie really did want to scream at this point, *I'm fine, Johnny, get on with it.*

Instead she said what she knew he wanted to hear, "I'm not contagious anymore."

Johnny leaned in and kissed her. Maggie stood and took Johnny by the hand. "Come with me, Johnny O'Brien, and I will let you have your way with me."

As they headed for the bedroom, Maggie wondered if nothing was going to be discussed tonight, that it was just Johnny wanting to spent time with his girl, who he hadn't seen in a week, that she had misread a carnal request to be alone, and that there was not going to be a marriage proposal. As Maggie slipped out of her blouse, it came over her that Johnny O'Brien, for all his wonderful attributes, was an enigma.

As they finished the last of the dishes, Johnny asked Maggie if they could talk in the living room. His tone was serious. It was a tone Maggie had never heard before. *This is it,* she thought. *He's going to do it.*

"Of course, Johnny," Maggie said as she took off her apron and offered her hand toward the sofa.

Johnny took a sip of his beer, seemed to gather himself, and then took Maggie's hand in his. "I want to—"

Maggie thought for sure he was going to ask her. Whatever was she thinking, doubting this wonderful man? This man who was about to ask for her hand in marriage. "The answer is yes, Johnny, yes," Maggie blurted out.

Johnny did a double take, his eyes saying, *What?*

Maggie felt a crimson blush flood her neck and cheeks. A sudden swirl of emotion flogged her insides. She thought she might get sick. She gathered herself in that split second as their eyes met. *Maintain your poise,* she told herself. She moved her hand back and forth in front of her face—*Forget that.* "You were saying," Maggie said.

"I want to tell you that I have a heart condition called hypertrophic cardiomyopathy." He went on to explain that he had inherited it from his father, who had died from the disease at forty-two. "And it can hit me any time after forty, maybe sooner."

"Oh, Johnny," Maggie said as she squeezed his hand, her heart suddenly clocking in her throat, her mind spinning on the verge of going haywire.

"Also," Johnny said in a defeated voice, "I can pass it on to my progeny."

Maggie said in as brave a voice as she could muster, "If you ask me, I will say yes."

"Maggie, I have never loved or will ever love anyone like you, but I would never forgive myself if I passed this incurable heart condition on to our child."

Our child, Maggie thought. Oh how she would like nothing more than to have a child with this beautiful, intriguing, perplexing man.

"What about adoption?" Maggie heard the desperateness in her voice.

Johnny put his beer on the side table and folded his arms across his chest. "No, Maggie; I am never going to marry."

Maggie felt her hands trembling and clasped her fingers together as though praying. The room seemed to be spinning around her. Johnny was now a blur; her hopes and dreams seemed an illusion. But she was not ready to quit yet. She must hang on and fight the urge to shake Johnny by the shoulders and knock some sense into him. She would make the best of the rest of the evening, and in the morning after things had settled down, Maggie would restate her case in regard to their marriage.

Somewhere deep in the recesses of her subconscious mind, that little voice was being ignored. A voice that was whispering, *He's not who you thought he was. He was never who you thought he was.*

In bed that night, Maggie made love to Johnny with a clinging desperateness as though holding on to him and her dreams for dear life.

As the morning light peeked through the blinds, Maggie turned on her side and faced Johnny, who was lying on his back, fingers laced behind neck, eyes staring vacantly at the ceiling. "I want to be with you,

Johnny. I want to take care of you if need be. I want to love you for the rest of your life, however long that is to be."

Johnny rolled over and faced Maggie, his scratchy red-streaked eyes with such a lost, faraway look. "Maggie, you deserve a real life with your own family, your own children." He brought his arm around her neck and brought Maggie in close, their faces inches apart. He started to speak and drew himself back, a hand on her shoulder. "You deserve a full life, a happy life ... and I can't offer you that."

"Johnny, don't do this. Please. Don't."

He looked at her, and in his gaze she saw the uselessness of it all. Why was he being so damn stubborn? Didn't he understand she would stand by him through it all? She would be with him for every moment he had left on this great Earth, no questions asked. Now, she had a taste, a big bitter mouthful, of what it felt like to be on the other end of it. "You're being selfish, Johnny." There, she said what she had been thinking and did not want to take it back.

"Selfish?" He burrowed his brow so that his eyes seemed like an angry slit slashed across his face. It was a new look.

"Yes, selfish," Maggie said in a rising voice. "How about thinking about it from my point of view?"

"Who the hell are you to call me selfish?" Johnny said as he untangled himself from the sheets and stood at the side of the bed naked. He looked so un-Johnny in that moment. The face twisted in an angry scowl as he lifted his underwear off the floor and slipped into them. His movements, as he fumbled into his clothes, no longer smooth and easy, but herky-jerky like an angry robot. "I've been living with this condition since I was ten years old."

Maggie flung herself out of bed and stood there in her nakedness staring daggers at Johnny. "And I offered to take care of you for as long as we would have together."

Everything had changed. They had taken this to a dangerous place. At that moment, Maggie's love had turned to something bordering on a strong dislike. "Say something," she demanded.

"I'm leaving."

"Oh," Maggie said as she wiped a drool of spittle off her mouth.

"That's right; walk away from it. Walk away from me and back to your mother. That's what you been doing all your life, isn't it?"

Johnny shot a look at Maggie that made it clear she had crossed a big boundary—a no-return zone.

As he walked out of the room, Maggie turned, still not wearing a stitch of clothes, and looked him squarely in the eyes. "I will be returning to California in the next couple of weeks." Her voice was so utterly cool and detached that she wondered momentarily if it had come from her.

After Johnny left, Maggie contacted Timmy Hite, the manager of the Raw Bar, and gave him two weeks' notice. Timmy asked what had brought this on, but Maggie only said, "Heading back west."

She spent all day Sunday in a mournful stupor, all the while refusing to give in to the urge to cry her eyes out. Later that night, when Nora returned, Maggie explained that she and Johnny had broken up, and she was heading out west.

"What happened, Maggie?" They were in Maggie's bedroom.

"Johnny ... oh God ... Nora," Maggie said as the tears she had been holding back came in a tidal wave.

Nora got Maggie to sit on the bed and sat next to her. She wrapped an arm around Maggie's shoulder, and Maggie leaned into her. Maggie cried and cried, and Nora held her steadfast.

Finally, Maggie said, "It's so sad, Nora, Johnny is not who I thought he was."

On Monday, Maggie dialed Johnny's business phone and left a message. "I said some things that I regret, Johnny. Give me a call, if nothing else so I can tell you in person."

But Tuesday came and went, and then by Wednesday, still no call, and a hurtful ire began to percolate inside Maggie.

For the remainder of the week, Maggie went through each day in a daze, somehow managing to get through work. She slept little, but no longer played the what-if game in her mind. She was hurt by his rejection, and then to top it off, he wouldn't even call her back. He definitely was not who she thought he was, the cowardly mama's boy. Not only had she burned a bridge with Johnny, but it was now reciprocal.

By Friday, Maggie had pulled herself together enough that if Johnny came in with the Friday-night basketball guys, she wouldn't fall apart; at least that's what she told herself. She didn't know how she would react if she saw him. Would he ignore her, or act polite in a reserved way that told her it was over? She didn't know if she could handle that look from him. The finality of it all.

But none of them came. Timmy said they were refurbishing the hardwood floor, and the gym was closed for the next two weeks.

Meanwhile, Nora's sister, Linda, was looking for not only a job but a place to stay. "It's like providence had you fetched back to Bethesda," Nora said to Maggie a couple of day before her departure. They were sitting on the sofa, sharing a bottle of Cabernet. "And now providence is making it easy for you to go back west."

The day before her departure, Maggie had contacted the Endless Summer, but they had no openings. Even so, she had some money saved and decided to head back to Manhassa Beach and figure it out.

Maggie then went to the Raw Bar to get her paycheck and ran into an old beau who transferred to WJ Maggie's senior year. He had been the opposite of Johnny, an unreliable pot-smoking lank of surfer dude, and by his casual stoner manner, he didn't appear to have changed one bit. In high school, Maggie had been drawn by his indifferent air. "A joint a day keeps the doctor away." He was a cool, slick character named Chick Silver, who wore a shark's tooth around his neck.

Chick was driving "my lime-green machine," a VW van, cross country, to Southern California, with a side trip to Mexico to buy five kilos of marijuana to resell across the border. And in her moment of depressed anger at Johnny O'Brien, Maggie decided to change her life's trajectory. She knew it made no sense what she was about to do, but she motioned to a booth. "Let's talk."

Chick raised his finger as if to say, "Just a moment." He tapped an empty pitcher, sitting on the bar. "Timmy, refill with two mugs."

Maggie sat across from Chick, who filled their mugs. "Want company, Chick?" There was a hollow ring to her voice, but Maggie didn't care.

Chick looked into Maggie's eyes to ascertain if she was serious. She made a face—*Well?*

"*Yeaaah*," Chick said. "Hell, yeah."

Next day, Maggie sold her car at a used-car lot and hit the road with Chick, each mile farther from Johnny's magnetic pull.

First night on the road, at a rest area on I-81 south of Roanoke, they ate peanut butter sandwiches and washed them down with lukewarm cans of Coke. As the sky was dying in a plush of violet, dusk fell over the land, the pine trees that lined both sides of the interstate like shadowy silhouettes.

They were the only vehicle, other than a semi parked off to the side of the exit ramp. After eating, Chick lit a fat doobie that they shared three tokes each.

The moon had risen over the trees to provide a slant of moonlight, and there was silence all around other than the occasional *whooshing* rumble of a truck on the highway. And then without a word, Maggie reached into her purse, removed a packet of condoms and tilted her head toward a mat in the back of the seatless shell. Chick looked at the condoms as if to say, *We don't need these, do we?* Maggie made a face back—*No arguments.*

Still in silence, they undressed, Maggie slipping out of her shorts and panties, then her T-shirt and, lastly, her bra. In the moody darkness, Maggie could sense a vibration of desire coming from Chick as he fumbled the condom on.

Maggie lay on her back and spread her legs. Chick slipped his long, lean body on top of hers. Her lips opened to his, and his tongue found hers, while his free hand cupped a breast, both of which were full and drawn up, the nipples stiff as door knockers.

By the time Chick entered her, Maggie was in full pant, and she screwed the bejesus out of him. After the missionary position, she finished it off with her on top, grinding and thrusting as though possessed, trying to fornicate Johnny O'Brien out of her mind.

Afterward, Maggie rolled off Chick onto her back, Chick laying there, fingers laced behind his neck, a grin of sexual contentment plastered across his face. He had the quintessential surfer look with white-blond hair, light blue eyes, and perpetual take-it-as-it-comes expression.

"Doobie time, Chick," Maggie said in an edgy voice.

Chick sat up and reached for a duffel bag at his feet. He lit a joint, lay back down, and took a deep, satisfying drag. After two tokes each, Chick snuffed out the joint, and soon after he fell asleep, chin tucked into neck above the shark's tooth.

In high school, Chick had told Maggie that the shark's tooth was his good luck charm. "Wards off evil spirits," he told her, doobie clamped in the corner of his mouth, index and middle finger rubbing the tooth as if trying to garner good fortune.

While dating Johnny, Maggie had only smoked grass a few times at parties. Johnny didn't smoke, and she always felt guilty about doing it in his company. But now with surfer dude, Maggie found herself escaping in the weed, and away from the memories of Johnny O'Brien.

While gentle snores wheezed out of Chick, Maggie got dressed and sat back up in the front passenger seat. There was something reckless going on with her, not only in the down-and-dirty sexual intercourse, but in Maggie packing up her clothes and leaving on the spur of the moment with a character like Chick.

As the moon slid behind a cloud, darkness draped everything in Maggie's purview. A breeze picked up, and a sudden, light rain began to fall, *tap-tapping* the roof of the van. There was change in the air.

CHAPTER 8

After six circuitous days on the road with stops in such places as Cradle Hollow, Tennessee; Conway, Arkansas; and Clinker, Texas; Maggie and Chick crossed the border into Santo Luis, Mexico.

Along the way, Maggie had resisted Chick's sexual advances. "I'm still trying to recover from the last time," she said a few nights into the journey. And farther on, "Not in the mood, Chick," Maggie said in a disgruntled tone. By this point, the only reason she was still with him was to return to California, and also curiosity about venturing into the non-touristy part of Mexico, warts and all.

It seemed Maggie had uncovered all the layers to Chick there were. He had not progressed since high school; in fact, he seemed even more of a ding-a-ling than she had remembered. "Can't wait 'til we get to Zuma Beach, and I tiptoe in the pocket of a monster tube, yeeaah." But she needed something to fill the void after Johnny, and a loser like Chick seemed to suit her present mood.

Also affecting her state of mind was the fact that she had missed her period the day before they departed, and was Maggie ever thankful for insisting on Chick wearing a condom. If pregnant, she wanted to be absolutely certain that it was Johnny's. She couldn't imagine carrying Chick's child.

Not taking her birth control pills had reached its fruition, almost as though her subconscious mind had realized what the conscious mind had not. Maggie knew two things: If the child was a boy; she would name him John; and, second, she would take the child to a cardiologist to see if Johnny's heart condition had been inherited.

El Rancho, Chick told Maggie as they drove down a dusty dirt road, was run by a man named Don Pilar, who lived with his niece Maya and her teenage son, Eduardo. "This is 160 acres of primo land," Chick said as they approached a ranch-style farmhouse with an exposed beam-and-timber-post porch. On the house's left side, extending past the porch, was a bump-out with an adobe facade. An apple tree and a couple of scrubby-looking mesquite trees offered spotty shade to the dirt yard where chickens scattered from the approaching van. Chick lifted a finger to his left to a cornfield. "A marijuana patch is stashed in the middle of those stalks."

Don Pilar was standing on the porch, hands on hips as if he was the owner of the sun. He had the squinty look of a wily coyote, a take-no-quarter sort of man of an indeterminable age. He could have been anywhere from fifty to eighty. Short and dark, the old man gave the impression of resilience, as though he had endured many things in this life.

At his side were Maya, a squatty, round woman in a wrinkled white blouse and faded blue skirt, and Eduardo, a tall, dark-haired youth wearing a purple print shirt and jeans. They were in a valley surrounded by brown hills in the distance.

As they emerged from the van, all eyes were on Maggie, suspicious eyes that said, "No outsiders." Don Pilar raised his hand for them to stop. He then lifted an eyebrow in Chick's direction and pointed his chin to his left.

On the side of the porch, the old man leaned forward, and spoke in a muffled voice to Chick, who nodded twice.

Chick came over to Maggie and said, "He says you have to leave."

Maggie looked at Chick—*What?*

"I'll drive you into the little town we passed through," Chick said, jerking his thumb over his shoulder toward the dirt road, "a ways back and come back to get you pronto after it all goes down, three days tops."

Maggie squinted a look at Chick—*Doofus*—and then walked right up to Don Pilar. She stood in front of him in cutoffs and a white T-shirt. "Mi nombre es Maggie, y no hablo, especialmente a los federales." She brought her index finger to her mouth in a sign of silence and tilted her head toward Don Pilar. It was a tilt of respect.

"Hmm." Don Pilar looked Maggie over, letting his eyes roam from her shapely, bare legs, to her hips, up to her stuffed shirt, the natural curves of her body tightening the right parts, two distinctive well-formed parts. His expression changed from disapproval to a flash of curious sexual indulgence to that of avuncular acceptance. He smiled a thin, knowing smile. "Okay," he said with a nod. "Te quadas."

Don Pilar led Maggie by the hand over to the front porch and introduced Maya and Eduardo to her. Maggie smiled and raised her hand in greeting.

They stared at Maggie, before Don Pilar told them to say hello. "Hola," they said in unison.

"Somos bunos?" Chick said to Don Pilar.

"Sí." Don Pilar cleared his throat to indicate new subject. "Dinero," he said, rubbing his thumb over his fingers.

Chick asked to see the marijuana with a "pretty please" expression.

Don Pilar threw a look over his shoulder at his nephew, who disappeared behind the house.

After a few minutes, the boy returned with a bulging khaki-colored duffel bag.

Don Pilar opened a zipper down the length of the bag and emptied a pile of small brown bags wrapped in plastic bags. He then offered his hand toward the bags.

Chick got down on his haunches and pulled out a brown bag and took a whiff. He did this on two more bags. He then smiled a big toothy grin and asked Don Pilar if this was from last year's crop.

"Si," the old man said. "It has been stored in a cool dry place and has lost none of its potency."

Chick stood and nodded. "Okay," he said. "Uno momento."

At the back of the van, Chick rooted around for a bit and then returned with a fat wad of crisp twenty-dollar bills. Don Pilar counted the money and then offered a sideways grin to Chick. "Bueno."

Don Pilar held the money over his shoulder. "Maya," he commanded.

Maya took the money and went inside the house. Don Pilar told

Chick that he and Maggie were welcome to join them for dinner. He then asked Chick if he was crossing the border as usual.

"Sí," Chick said. He asked if Maggie could stay back while he crossed on foot and then come back for—

"What?" Maggie interrupted, staring daggers at Chick. "You didn't mention anything about this."

Chick explained, "Crossing the border into the States in a faded green VW bus with a shitload of dope is risky." He lifted his chin toward the van. "Look at that and put us in it," he said. "Do we, me especially, look like tourists?"

His tone was unhurried and thoughtful, and Maggie was starting to understand that Chick was savvy when it came to his drug dealing.

Chick also explained that after crossing the border, he would stash the duffel bag in a "very safe spot," before returning. "Twenty miles up and twenty miles back, three days."

Chick turned his focus back at Don Pilar, who had a thin smile creasing the corner of his lips.

"No hay problema," the old man said.

CHAPTER 9

Don Pilar waited until everyone had entered the house. He looked up the dirt road and then into a scrubby thicket along the road—nothing. It would soon be a dangerous time of year, his marijuana crop coming to harvest in a few months. There were men, ruthless men, who would stop at nothing to steal his prize.

He had lived and worked this land since he was fourteen years old, coming here with his mother during the Mexican Revolution, when his father was killed fighting for the División del Norte under the leadership of the great Pancho Villa, in the taking of Mexico City.

El Rancho was originally owned by young Don's mother's brother, Uncle Alvaro, a confirmed bachelor, who soon took his young nephew under his wing. Uncle Alvaro grew corn and cotton and had an apple orchard on the back of the property. There were difficult times over the years, when the droughts and boll weevils swept across the land. One season they all would have perished if not for the apples and meager ration of corn.

When Uncle Alvaro dropped dead in the field during harvest of the corn, a field hand helped carry the body to the far corner of the apple orchard. Don told the hand to return to work. He then dug a deep grave, with his heartbroken mother looking on. Don had promised his uncle, when he died, not to spend money on a funeral, and for Don to bury him on the ranch with only his mother in attendance. "Es mio camino" (It is my way), the uncle had said.

After the last stone marker had been placed, Don's mother said a prayer, and then they both returned to the field.

After the harvest, Don implemented changes that his uncle would not consider, such as contour plowing, cover crops, and crop rotation, all of which he had read about in agricultural journals. He also brought to the ranch two cousins, on his father's side, who lived nearby, to supervise field hands during harvest and assist with other chores as needed. Don Pilar also introduced a new and much more profitable crop.

As the years went on, Don's mother passed, and he took in his widowed niece, Maya, and her infant son. Like his uncle, Don Pilar stayed unmarried. And, also like his uncle, from time to time he frequented the *puna casa* in the village to satisfy his one weakness— *deseo sexual*. But unlike his uncle, he became a wealthy man, but a man who never displayed his wealth, a man who lived a simple, unassuming life, a life that drew little attention.

Inside the house, Don welcomed his guests and offered a seat. The drug dealer sat wearily on the sofa, his long body seeming to sigh with relief, but the woman had an inquisitive look in her eyes and motioned toward the backyard.

"Si," Don said with a lift of his chin. "Enjoy the view." He was proud of his land and his home that he and Maya had maintained and improved upon: the exposed wood beams and plank wood floor and tongue-and-groove walls, all that he had painstaking installed over time; the starkness of the wood was offset by paintings of agrarian life—an apple orchard with field hands picking fruit, a pasture of horses backdropped by snow-peaked mountains, and a field of bright wildflowers, red and gold.

An intricately woven braided carpet covered most of the main room, which flowed to the kitchen, where the aroma of beef and vegetables emanated from a cast iron pot on the stove that Maya tended. This was her domain, which she had refurbished by herself, installing rough-hewn cabinets and terra-cotta floor with an array of cooking utensils, cast iron skillets, and enamel cookware hanging from the wall.

Don approached the double door that opened to a half-moon-shaped flagstone patio; beyond it was the garden lined with rows of leafy green plants and tomatoes, and a section of herbs, also Maya's domain along with help from her son. Past the garden was the apple orchard.

The young Americano woman was on the patio, looking off to her left to the barn. Don Pilar had rehabbed the barn for curing after his uncle died, installing a second-story A-frame constructed of timber planks with two rows of slatted air vents at six-foot intervals along the side to provide the proper ventilation.

H saw the quizzical expression on the young woman's face as though there was something forbidding about this windowless building of dull gray adobe and timber; its only access a heavy-duty metal door secured by a series of large double hasps with a heavy chain running vertical through them and secured by a large lock.

Don approached her and said, "Te gusta, ¿no?" (You like, no?)

She appeared so taken by the vista that she hadn't noticed Don Pilar standing behind her. She told him that it was beautiful, before she stole another look at the barn.

"Ahh," Don Pilar said, "commerce is a necessity to maintain beauty." He shrugged as if to say *that's the way it is,* before Maya came out and announced dinner.

Don Pilar took his seat at the head of the table, to his right the young woman, Maggie, on his other side Chick, the Americano drug dealer. They seemed an odd pair, Chick reminding Don of some renegade living here and there, buying and selling his weed. The girl, Maggie, seemed more like his impression of the traditional American woman: smart, assertive, but with a look of someone in transition, as though she had left some trying experience—another man?—and traveled with Chick on impulse.

But this woman had stood up for herself, speaking fluent Spanish when she pleaded her case with Don to stay. He liked that. And he liked her, not just the beauty, but her espíritu. And he saw that Maya liked having her, another female under the same roof. Maya had even placed the embroidered tablecloth of butterflies, flowers, and birds, which Don's mother had made years ago, over the rectangular table.

Besides a porcelain bowl of beef stew, there was a breadbasket of corn muffins, and a wooden salad bowl with green leaf lettuce and colorful vegetables from the garden.

Don Pilar extended his arms to take hold of Maggie and Chick's hands. "Gracias," he said as hands grasped hands. Don Pilar said a short grace, and then the food was passed around the table.

The stew was tender and succulent, as was the salad, which Maya had tossed with honey-lime vinaigrette. His niece had been a great asset; Don couldn't imagine life on El Rancho without her.

Conversation was minimal during the meal, save Don Pilar asking Maggie if she wanted another serving, which she said yes to, and Chick starting a business conversation with Don Pilar about crossing the border, which he looked upon with a scolding frown.

Also during dinner, Maya offered a meek smile in Maggie's direction, a smile that said, "I hope you appreciate my table setting and my cooking." Maggie returned the look with a beaming acknowledgment. A woman's company for Maya seemed to bring out the best in not only her cooking but in lifting her spirit.

Although, Don Pilar and Maya had accepted Maggie's presence, Eduardo still kept his distance, as he ate with a controlled vigor as though trying not to give away his hunger. He reminded Don of himself at that age. Since Chick and Maggie's arrival, the boy had not spoken one word. But that was Eduardo's way, someone who was comfortable and confident in his silence. And though still wary of Chick, after having known him from the past, Eduardo seemed even more so of the young woman Chick brought with him. A slanty, sideways glance when he thought she wasn't looking.

The woman Don had initially been leery of, but had been won over with her mastery of the native tongue and her confidence in her own skin. Skin that Uncle Don Pilar had examined with a look of admiration, of something rare, a beautiful white woman from gringo land up north.

CHAPTER 10

Since their arrival, Chick had entered into business mode. The surfer-dude act was replaced by the quiet, observant young man in the midst of a big score. He acted respectfully to Don Pilar, deferring to him, standing patiently in the living room upon entry, and only sitting when Don Pilar offered a hand toward the sofa, and waiting to be asked to be seated at the dinner table. Also, he had a standup quality when asking, very politely, to see the marijuana before paying. Yes, old doofus surfer dude was gone, and a young, shrewd drug dealer in his stead.

Maggie, who had minored in Spanish in college, had asked Chick fifty miles from the Mexican border if he spoke the language. "Three years of Spanish in high school and two more at MC," Chick said in reference to the local community college. "By eleventh grade, I knew dope trips to Mexico may well be in my future." He made a face to indicate that's the way it is. "He aprendido español."

And well he should know the language, Maggie thought as she took a clean, wet plate from Maya at the kitchen sink and wiped it. This land south of the border is no place for any signs of stupidity or uncertainty. Chick had told Maggie on the road trip that where they were going was bandito land. "Really," Maggie had said, in a tone of curiosity. "Yes indeed," Chick said. "More than a few men have died in disagreements over weed." They were driving through the coastal plains of East Texas, a windy river on one side and grasslands the other. "This purchase could set me … us," he said, correcting himself, "up for a good long while."

Maggie considered this a roguish adventure, an escape from the gravitational pull of one Johnny O'Brien, the only one who had ended a courtship with her. For once the shoe was on the other foot, and Maggie hadn't liked it one damn bit. Why wouldn't he marry her, when she had offered to do it? Why wouldn't he let her take care of him in sickness and in health? She would have gone the entire distance for Johnny, but it was not to be. They were not to be. And Maggie would never forget the look on his face when she had told him he was selfish. And then the coup de grâce, when she said, "Walk away from me and back to your mother. That's what you been doing all your life, isn't it?"

Johnny's shocked expression—*Who are you?*—turned to hurtful resentment. At that moment it was over.

But with the distance of time and space came a certain understanding that Johnny, in his own way, was telling himself that he was doing this in Maggie's best interest, not wanting to saddle her with a husband on a constant death watch. And passing on the disease to his child, whom she was already carrying and may well have inherited Johnny's heart condition. But part of her did wonder if he used it as an excuse, to stay free and unencumbered with another woman in his life. He doted so on his mother.

The loss of a father at a young age, and if that was not enough, the heart condition that would shorten Johnny's life, seemed to have formed an inseparable bond between mother and son. And if Maggie had married Johnny, would she always be the third wheel, coexisting with Mary O'Brien under the same roof?

Even so, part of Maggie wanted to hightail it back to Bethesda and let Johnny know he was going to be a father, but another, stronger part told her to hold up. Their fight had changed the paradigm; he was no longer the perfect man of her dreams, but a flawed one, and one whom she still thought a coward. If the situation were reversed, she would have married him in a heartbeat. And he might resent her getting pregnant; Maggie could envision the look on his face.

Then there was Maggie's side of it—he had flat out turned her down. He'd had his chance to marry her, and another rejection was something she would not be able to handle. *Yes, better off they go their separate ways,* Maggie told herself, as she suddenly felt a queasy, gurgling sensation in the pit of her stomach.

CHAPTER 11

Chick had been gone for two days, and tomorrow was his scheduled return date. After Chick had left, Maya offered to share her room with Maggie, who hesitated for only a moment before accepting. The three bedrooms were down a hallway off the living room, with Don Pilar's at the end, Eduardo's next, and Maya's at the front of the house. Maggie and Maya slept in a queen-size bed, and it was the first time she had shared a bed with a woman since she was a little girl and had slept with her mother when her father was away on business trips.

There had been an almost immediate bond between these two women from such different worlds. Maya was rather plain-looking, a peasant woman making do in this rural, masculine world of earth and sky. There was a quiet hospitality about this round brown woman, whom Maggie sensed from the beginning was pleased to have the company of another female: the shy smiles at the first dinner, tending to Maggie that first night when the queasy stomach turned into full-blown vomiting in the front yard. Maya had helped her into the bathroom—Don Pilar and Chick powwowing on the patio unaware—and washed Maggie's face.

And then the next morning when Chick departed, two packs strapped on his back, he threw a gritty look over his shoulder at Maggie as he walked off, disappearing into a thicket of mesquite trees and scrubby brush off the dirt road. Maya took Maggie's hand in hers, her warm touch letting Maggie know she was not alone.

For the next two days, Maggie seamlessly nestled herself into the daily routine on the ranch. She assisted Maya, who was a knowledgeable cook, in the kitchen, collected eggs from the chicken coop next to the barn, which she still hadn't been inside, and tried to help Maya weeding and collecting vegetables in the garden, but she tired quickly. Maya insisted Maggie rest under the shade of a mimosa tree on the edge of the patio, while she finished in the garden. Maggie's first instinct was to decline, but she realized that she was now responsible for her future progeny. She felt a strong desire to have this child, to nurture him—she sensed it was a boy—into adulthood. Never once did she consider an abortion; the thought of it repulsed her.

Maggie tried not to think about the future and what it held for her and her child. With no family, other than some distant cousins she met once as a child, Maggie Meyers was alone in this world.

Her parents' deaths had left a scar, an invisible scar. First there was the hurt and sense of unfairness, and after her mother's death, the survivor instincts kicked in. Maggie had always had been adept at handling pressure and stress, some innate gift she was born with to keep striving forward. But along the way, tiptoeing in like a thief in the night emerged a pragmatic hardness to always look out for herself first. What was lost in this stealthy transaction she never considered.

Now the paradigm had shifted again, and not so subconsciously this time, for the growing embryo inside was not only Maggie's number one priority, but had altered her perception of those in her life. Now she worried for Chick, that gritty expression on his departure she never could have imagined him to possess. It was a look of one entering into enemy territory, a boy in foreign woods.

On Chick's last night, he and Maggie were ensconced in their sleeping bags in the van. He had told Maggie that he had made this trek three times in the last five years, but things were growing more dangerous, and there were not only the Federales to worry about but banditos in the valley, who would not only take your goods but your life. "This is my last one," he said. There was a tone of fait accompli in his voice. "What's the old song," Chick said as he rolled over on his side and faced Maggie, "'Whatever will be, will be'?"

CHAPTER 12

Maggie woke with a start. She had dreamed that Chick had been caught by a gang of banditos on horseback. Maya had told her of such desperados, called Los Fantasmas de la Noche, Night Ghosts. She dreamt Chick had been stripped of his clothing, scalped of his blond hair, and hung on a lone mesquite tree in the high desert. Hands tied behind his back, he rocked gently back and forth, his feet inches from the ground, in dead silence. It all seemed so real: Chick's eyes wide open like twin blue stars, his stubbly head leaking blood, and his long, lanky body a frightful pale white as though death had robbed his corpse of his beautiful golden tan.

It had been a week since Chick had departed. Don Pilar had driven into Santo Luis and made a few inquiries with his contacts and had heard nothing of an arrest of a gringo. "Banditos," he told Maggie, "one could never be sure of." He shrugged as if to say that's the way things are around here.

Maggie wasn't certain if he had been captured and killed as in her dream or if he decided to go off on his own. For Chick's sake, she hoped it was the latter.

Maggie sat up in bed. As if on cue the morning sickness invaded her stomach. Maya got the pot that they kept under the bed, and Maggie heaved a trickling stream of vomit. When she had finished, Maya wiped Maggie's mouth with a wet cloth and helped her back into bed.

It took ten minutes of complete stillness, lying flat on her back, for Maggie to feel well enough to get out of bed. She got dressed and went into the kitchen and insisted on helping Maya prepare breakfast. They went through this drill every morning: Maya raising her hands for Maggie to stop, Maggie cracking eggs in a bowl and whisking them, and Maya saying softly, "No demasiado, Maggie, no demasiado" (Not too much, Maggie, not too much).

Maya had told Maggie that morning sickness was a good sign that everything was doing well in regard to the pregnancy. "I was sick every morning and then also sometimes during the day until the second trimester," she told Maggie one day in the garden. Maya had then straightened herself from hoeing weeds and said in a confident tone, a tone Maggie had never heard from her before, "You must not try to leave."

Maggie stopped snipping leaves off a tomato plant; in the distance the brown hills reminded her of camel humps. She looked at Maya, who placed her hand on Maggie's stomach and said, "If not for yourself, Maggie, then the niño." Maya put her hand on Maggie's face. "I will look after you."

Soon the days turned into weeks, and then by the start of the second trimester, the morning sickness had departed. Maggie not only helped Maya around the house and garden, but there was another chore she wanted to participate in. For the last two weeks, day laborers arrived every morning; they had already picked all the corn, but left the stalks for cover of the marijuana.

She waited until after dinner and went out to the patio where Don Pilar enjoyed his one cigar of the day, sitting and looking out past the garden and orchard at the inscrutable brown hills off in the distance.

"Excusa, Don Pilar," Maggie said as she came up to his side.

Don Pilar stood and placed a chair so it faced his seat. "Sit," he said.

"May I assist you in the harvest of marijuana?"

"So you want to help, eh …" Don Pilar studied Maggie carefully with his sly gaze. "Maybe learn something too, huh?"

Don Pilar turned his cigar in his fingers. "This is my one indulgence. Cohiba cigar from Cuba, world-class smoke." Don Pilar's eyebrows flared, a smile lurking in the corner of his mouth. "A friend of Fidel's bodyguard made them by hand. The rest, as they say, is history." He took a deep inhale of his Cohiba, held it for a moment, and exhaled ringed puffs of smoke.

The old man stared sleepily at Maggie, eyelids at half-mast as though pondering some great decision. He then smiled broadly and brought his finger to his mouth and tilted his head toward Maggie, mimicking her the first day they met. Though not a tilt of respect, it was a tilt of acknowledgment. *You are one of us.*

CHAPTER 13

The first day Maggie joined the marijuana harvest, Don Pilar told her to watch and learn. "You are a smart girl," he told her as he nodded hello to his assembling field hands. "You will pick this up quickly: harvesting, cutting, trimming, and drying." He gave a faint smile and said in a soft, kindly voice, "Three, four months?"

"Going on four," Maggie whispered.

Don Pilar glanced at Maggie's stomach. "Nothing shows yet," he said, "but you have the niño to think about."

The field hands were broken up into groups, each with a specific duty. One group snipped off all the large leaves to the stem, another followed by trimming off the leaf tips that were all around the buds. At this point Don Pilar then examined the buds with a magnifying glass. "Bueno, tricomas medio ámbar, medio nublado" (Good, trichome half amber, half cloudy). All the while he reminded the men to be gentle when handling the plant.

Another group of hands carefully cut off each branch at the stock, and the fourth group came behind placing the buds into paper grocery bags.

And just as Chick had told Maggie, the marijuana field was smack in the middle of the cornfield. She was surprised how big the marijuana plants were, up to seven feet high.

On the second day, Maggie snipped leaves off the plants for two hours, and then Don Pilar told her that was enough for the day. The next day, very carefully she trimmed off the leaf tips.

At first the men seemed a bit shy and uncomfortable working with the gringo woman, but soon they seemed at ease, some of the younger men stealing a glance of admiration at Maggie before returning to the task at hand. It was a respectful look, but also there was something wild in it, like a half-tamed animal that still had the potential to revert back to nature.

This was a different way of life out here in the Mexican badlands. Many of these men lived day-to-day, sometimes going hungry, Maggie imagined, and sometimes she wondered if they didn't do things they normally wouldn't to stay alive.

Toward the end of Maggie's third and last day in the marijuana field, Don Pilar took her to the barn. At the metal door entrance, he took hold of the huge combination lock that secured the chains running through the vertical hasps. Don Pilar looked to his left and then his right, where he spotted one of the field hands off to their side, watching.

There was a hunger in the eyes of this man, Charo, a predatory hunger that sent a chill through Maggie when he had looked at her earlier in the day. It was a flashing glance, but she caught a squinty-eyed look of avaricious lust—a naked look of a man with nothing to lose. *I will have my way with you, and then slit your throat for the fun of it, woman.* All of that in a glance.

Why was a hulking, fearsome hombre like this working with this crew of quiet, soulful men anywhere in age from late teens to forty? This man with a constant five o'clock shadow of dark stubble, beady eyes, and stained, crooked teeth was an outlier, this wolf in the hen house, and Maggie being the hen. Whatever was Don Pilar thinking, hiring him? Or was Don Pilar unaware? The old man was on top of everything when it came to his ranch and the people working it. Maggie remembered an old saying: "Keep your friends close and your enemies closer."

Don Pilar lifted his chin to Charo, his expression saying *vamoose*.

Charo offered a crooked grin, his eyes two slits like a cagey desert predator. "El Jefe, do you need help?"

"No," Don Pilar said. "Now leave me."

Charo was still holding the grin, looking for all the world like a badass desperado in a B movie. He nodded, turned slowly, and walked away.

Don Pilar kept his eyes on the man until he disappeared back into the cornfield.

Maggie squinted as her eyes adjusted to the dusky darkness inside the barn, the only light from the open doors and the overhead louvers. Marijuana plants were hanging from rows of rope strung like clotheslines, running the length of the barn. Don Pilar walked Maggie up and down the barn, the proud El Jefe displaying his weedy fortune. Stored on shelves along the walls were mason jars filled with marijuana buds. "They must stay in the jars for a few weeks to reach the proper curing stage," he said as he lifted a jar off the shelf and inspected it. He nodded his approval and said, "Proper drying and curing is essential to increase the potency by separating oxygen from the THC."

Maggie asked a few questions, and Don Pilar answered in full and with a knowledge that would have made a biochemist proud. This man knew marijuana.

Back outside the barn, Don Pilar closed the doors and looked left and looked right. He ran the heavy chain through the hasps—four in all—and pulled the chain tight and secured it with the lock.

When Maggie and Don Pilar returned to the marijuana field, the field hands were finishing up the last patch to be harvested.

The men were cutting, trimming, and bundling with energetic care. They had worked hard, with payday on the horizon. Charo was cutting stalks at the base with a long, sharp knife. *Cling, cling,* went the blade through the plants. When he had finished, he caught Maggie's eye and smiled the scariest smile she had ever been the recipient of, even worse than the first time he had leered at her. There was something evil and foreboding about this hombre. Maggie would be glad when the harvest was over and Charo had left El Rancho.

After the harvest was completed, including packing the finished product in carefully weighed and tightly packed plastic bags, Don Pilar had the crew of field hands over to the ranch for a fiesta.

Maggie and Maya prepped and cooked for three days in preparation, including Maya and Eduardo chasing down squawking chickens in the yard, Eduardo striking one on the head with a broom, and Maya grabbing the dazed bird by the throat and whacking its head off with a hatchet on a tree stump. She killed three birds with ruthless efficiency, showing nary an ounce of emotion.

Eduardo, wearing rubber gloves, scalded the dead birds in a bucket of very hot water and then plucked the feathers. Maya and Maggie took the skinned birds into the kitchen, where Maya, with Maggie watching closely, gutted a bird, first cutting off the talons and then removing the insides. After Maya cleaned the first bird, Maggie did the next two, and by the end of cutting up the third, she had it down.

The day of the fiesta, Don Pilar sent one of the field hands out in his pickup, and he soon returned with a skinned pig, head and feet intact, stretched out on a tarp in the bed of the truck. As the man lifted the carcass out of the truck and slung it over his shoulder, it reminded Maggie of an elongated torso of a man who had been skinned and had his eyes removed—a blind pigman.

The pig was carried to a cinderblock pit that Eduardo had built. In the pit was a stack of mesquite wood stacked vertically, like a teepee.

Another hand took the tarp and a metal hand crank and skewer spit from the truck over to the pit. The pig was placed on the tarp. The two men, together, rammed the skewer into the rear of the dead animal until it came out through the chest. It seemed such a brutal, savage way to prepare a meal; and much like Maya decapitating the chickens, the men showed nary an ounce of emotion. In this faraway land, death seemed a way of life.

CHAPTER 14

When the last of the trays of food had been placed on a long table under the shade of a tarp strung atop bamboo poles, Maggie took a moment to admire her and Maya's work: platters of succulent pork strips stacked high from the pig that Eduardo had cooked, taco shells stuffed with ground beef and chicken, enchiladas, bowls brimming with produce from the garden, handmade corn chips and salsa dip, and pitchers of beer and margaritas.

The hands—there were sixteen men in attendance—had cleaned themselves up: shaven faces; clean, if worn, clothes; and looks on their faces like those of little boys at an amusement park awaiting their first ride. *But wait,* Maggie thought, as one man was missing—Charo.

The men served themselves quietly as they piled food on their plates. At the end of the line, they poured either a beer or margarita and a couple did both. Everyone ate standing up or sitting on the porch steps; only Don Pilar sat in a chair on the porch, a slant-eyed watchfulness about him. Maggie thought he would let himself relax after what he had described as a record harvest. Possibly he was concerned about the valuable weed in the barn or after he sold it. "Sólo el dinero Americano," he had told Maggie. He did not trust Mexican money.

She wondered where he kept his money and what he did with it all. They lived a very simple life here on the ranch with no indoor plumbing; there was a bathroom toilet, but the excrement was used as compost. A job that Eduardo was none too fond of, but one he did every week, with nose squished up and a sour look on his face. Though there was electricity provided by a generator on the side of the house, it was only run in the evening before lights out no later than ten. It was early September, and though the days had been scorchers, it cooled to a tolerable level in the evening.

Don Pilar must have amassed a small fortune. Chick had told Maggie that the old man had been "growing and selling good weed for decades." Don Pilar did drive into town on a weekly basis, and possibly he kept his money in a safety deposit box in a bank or stashed it somewhere on the property.

Maya had mentioned that any time now a big buyer was coming to purchase most of the marijuana. She said that Don Pilar was always concerned during this time. "Night Ghosts," she said with an edge in her voice.

Years ago, men on horseback had tried to rob Don Pilar, but he had been waiting for them up the dirt road, in a tree blind. Back then, Don Pilar had been a crack shot and had picked them off, killing three men and two horses, panicking the remaining horses, which bucked some of the riders, who ran for their lives back up the road from which they came. But that was a long time ago, and many of the banditos today were not alive when this happened, though they had heard the stories. "And," Maya added, "Don Pilar's vision is not so good anymore."

As the evening rolled on, the food eaten and the liquor drunk, the men began to loosen up. They talked among themselves, laughing and reliving the harvest. There was a trace of pride in their voices as though they were part of some great undertaking. Maggie overheard them mention Charo. "The fiesta is better without *la bestia*," one man said in a loud voice before catching himself and looking around to see if he had been overheard. Don Pilar glanced over at the remark, his blank expression revealing nothing.

Maggie thought *the beast* was a perfect name for Charo, a silent, sullen man with long, jet-black hair that he wore in braids. There was something prehistoric about him: thick jutting jaw, broad nose, and pronounced forehead.

After the last of the liquor was downed, the food eaten, and Maggie and Maya had finished the cleanup, dusk settled over the land, and with it the field hands departed. They crammed themselves into small battered cars and puttered off with full bellies and a sleepy-eyed alcohol-induced contentment.

But the evening was not over for Don Pilar, who was now sitting on the porch, in the darkness, with a rifle across his lap. He told the two women and Eduardo to go bed. Eduardo had gotten into the beer during the fiesta and volunteered in a slurred voice to stand guard with Don Pilar.

"Good night, nephew," Don Pilar said as he lifted his chin toward the door.

Tucked in bed next to Maya, Maggie asked why Don Pilar didn't get help guarding the marijuana. "He is stubborn—his one flaw," Maya said in a weary voice. "Also," she added, "he trusts no one other than family." Maya went on to say that there used to be more men cousins working on the ranch, but, "Some of them died, and some married and left. Now the only man left is still a boy."

Maggie went into the kitchen and removed a sharp paring knife from a drawer. "Just in case," she said under her breath as she returned to her room.

She tucked it under her pillow and rolled over on her side, listening for any sign of trouble. It was too quiet, not a chirp of a cricket, not a whisper of wind, not coyotes howling from the hills—quiet.

CHAPTER 15

An exhausted *thoot, thoot* sound stirred Maggie from a restless sleep. And then came the clop of horse hooves and the rumble of wheels on hard earth. Maggie and Maya bolted out of bed across the hall to Eduardo's empty room. At the hurried pat of footsteps on the front porch, they crawled out the back window of Eduardo's room, Maya in a sleeveless nightshirt and Maggie in her bra and panties. "Let's run to the orchard," Maggie said. "Uno momento—Eduardo," Maya said.

Crouched down at the side of the house, they watched shadowy figures hovering around the double doors to the barn. As Maggie reached for Maya's hand to lead her to the orchard, she felt a cold, hard tip on the back of her neck. "Ah, the sexy gringo bitch." A hand, a very strong hand, took hold of the back of Maggie's neck and jerked her up to a standing position.

"Turn around and look at me," the heavy voice demanded.

Maggie turned to see a face in white war paint save black streaks under and over and on both sides of the eyes—Night Ghost. It was the eyes, dark and foreboding eyes, that could only belong to one man— Charo. He was standing next to a smaller, shorter man with similar face paint and with a long bow and quiver strung across his chest and back.

Maggie felt her heart leap a beat as Maya made a run for the cornfield. The other man started for her, but Charo told him to stop. "Let the fat pig go," he said as he turned his slit eyes back on Maggie. "We going to have some fun tonight, bitch." He shoved Maggie toward the front yard, where more Night Ghosts were standing in a circle holding long knives at their side.

Closer to the circle, Maggie saw two bodies on the ground and knew before she saw the faces who they would have to be. The men looked at Maggie standing there so skimpily attired. A few had the same lustful look as Charo, but the others turned from looking at her as though embarrassed at what they saw. Maggie wondered if some of these masked men were field hands. The war paint and the darkness made it hard to tell for sure.

"This is what happens when *la bestia* hunts at night," Charo said in an amused tone, his sandpaper rough voice only adding to the terror ripping through Maggie. "Take a good look, bitch," Charo said pushing her so that Maggie stood over Eduardo's body in a pool of blood, a long slash mark across his bloodied throat. How young and innocent he looked, his mouth open in a small circle as though he were about to speak.

Don Pilar's corpse had two arrows to the heart. Charo bent over and yanked the arrows out.

Maggie felt suddenly ill and fought her body from vomiting. *Stay steady, stay strong,* she told herself. Hooting whoops and howls turned everyone's attention to the barn where the metal door had been breached. Charo ordered the men to load the marijuana on a horse-drawn wagon stationed up the dirt road.

As the men departed, Charo put his knife under Maggie's chin, causing her to raise her head. "In the house, gringo bitch. Charo gonna fuck you good ... before." He then let out a choppy hoarse laugh.

Maggie had to keep her wits and think out of the box. At the edge of the cornfield, she saw a round, shadowy figure. Maggie devised a quick plan and only hoped it would work.

Charo shoved Maggie into her bedroom, where before he could say anything, she removed her bra and turned to face him. Her breasts were full and firm, the dark nipples sticking straight out. As confidently as possible, she then removed her undies.

"Ooh," Charo grunted in a tone of carnal curiosity as he leaned forward to take a closer look. Maggie stepped back and sat on the bed and then lay on her back. "I have wanted you, *la bestia*, since the first time I saw you." She spread her legs and raised her knees. "Come eat my pussy and then have your way with me."

Maggie kept her eyes on Charo as he put his knife into the leather sheath on his belt and came to the foot of the bed. He removed a bandana from around his neck to reveal Chick's shark tooth hanging around his neck. "Blondie, he cry like little girl before ..." Charo drew his finger across his throat and let out another bloodcurdling laugh. "I eat and then fuck you good ... having fun, gringo bitch?" His dark eyes opened wide, a knowing look of a wild animal, a sinister smirk slashing his ghostly white face. "You think you fool me, with this act?" he said. "Where is it?"

Maggie was frozen stiff with fear. She literally could not move or say a word—frozen.

Charo shimmied up on the bed, his knees butting up against Maggie's buttock. He pinned her head off to the side with the heel of his hand and lifted the pillow. "Hah ... you sly cunt," he said as he waved the paring knife in her face.

"Charo will make you pay." He tossed the paring knife across the room and slapped Maggie with the heel of his hand across the face, causing her to see stars for an instant.

He placed his hands on her bare breasts and squeezed; a drop of milk dripped out of a nipple. "Yah," he roared.

Charo ran his hand over Maggie's stomach, which had a slight curve to it. He pushed his hand down, slowly applying more pressure. "You hiding Blondie's niño in here, bitch?"

He stuck out his long, coarse tongue. It was dark brown with a prominent ridge down the middle. "I eat you good," he said as he grabbed Maggie firmly by both her wrists and went down on her. He licked her vaginal opening with the tip of his tongue like a dog finishing a bowl.

As the tongue began to slowly penetrate deeper, Maggie saw Maya stealthy approaching Charo's rear with a pair of shearing scissors. Maggie groaned loudly as though enjoying the tongue. "Más adentro" (deeper), Maggie said. "Yes, yes."

Maya lunged forward, plunging the scissors deep into the side of Charo's neck. She pulled them out quickly as Charo brought a hand to his gashed neck; his eyes seemed prepared to launch from their sockets in shocked disbelief, as he let out a horrific scream, "Awwggg."

Maggie clamped her legs tight around Charo's waist, holding on with every bit of strength she could muster, as Maya clutched Charo's braids and jerked his head back, driving the scissors deep into his throat over and over again. There was a calmness about this brown, heavyset woman as she repeated this act, nary a bit of emotion on her expressionless face. It was no different than when she would slaughter a chicken. Blood was spurting out of Charo's neck in waves, and in rhythm with his heartless heart.

All the while Maggie kept her legs wrapped firmly around Charo's waist, as she watched the life drain out of him, the eyes glazed over as if to say, "What happened?"

Charo fell forward onto Maggie, who squirmed her way out from under him.

"Come, quickly, Maggie," Maya said as she took Maggie by the hand.

They scurried from the room, out the back door into the darkness of night, through the garden, to the orchard, and hid there until the morning sun lifted over the hills.

CHAPTER 16

During the night, Maggie and Maya had seen the smoke billowing up into the night sky, and they had heard the war whoops of the banditos. Maya had told Maggie that many people believed that the Night Ghosts are mixed-blood descendants of a nomadic Indian tribe that had lived in these hills for many centuries.

Maggie asked if some of the field hands were Night Ghosts. They were at the far end of the orchard, nearby the trickling splatter of a stream and the lonesome howl of a coyote the only sound audible. The faint scent of charred wood lingered in the air.

"For sure, one," Maya had said.

"They seemed like decent people, the field hands," Maggie said.

"One type of person when under the thumb, another with bow and arrow." They were sitting under the cover of an apple tree, and Maya reached up and picked one. "When they get together with their horses and their long bows, and put on war paint ..." She studied the apple for a moment and took a bite. Maya looked over her shoulder as a sudden breeze rustled through the treetops, her eyes unblinking like a cat deciding on its next move. "They revert back to their ancestors' past—Night Ghosts."

Maya went on to tell Maggie that many were probably feeling very guilty about their actions, "Until the next time they ride at night."

At dawn, Maggie and Maya returned to the property; the house was a smoldering heap, as was the barn. The bodies of Don Pilar and

Eduardo were gone, as was Charo's body. The pickup and Chick's van were still there.

Both women were barefoot, Maya in her nightshirt and Maggie naked. Behind the remains of the barn, Maya led Maggie to a metal storage bin. Inside were rubber gloves, boots, and overalls and denim shirts, all of which they put on.

They went to the house to see what was left. All that remained in the living room were the smoky remains of the sofa, a few ragged scorched sections of the beautiful braided carpet, and on the floor the painting of an apple orchard with field hands picking fruit backdropped by snow-peaked mountains that had somehow survived, lying glass side up. In the kitchen, a black cast iron frying pan appeared none the worse, shards of pottery were everywhere, and the stove was a melted hulk that brought to Maggie's mind the Wicked Witch having melted. A light mist of ash hung in the air.

In what was once the dining room, Maya bent down on her haunches and removed a square section of bricks, where the dinner table used to be. Underneath was an iron door with a handle.

Below them was a ladder that led to a space no more than ten by ten with a six-foot ceiling and plastered walls. Maya removed a heavy-duty flashlight from the wall. In the back was a black steel combination safe. Inside it was more American currency than Maggie had ever laid eyes on: stacks and stacks of twenties and fifties in plastic bags. Maya handed Maggie two bags: one twenties, the other fifties. "Maggie, drive far away and forget this land of constant sorrow."

PART 2

The Road Less Traveled

CHAPTER 17

As Maggie drove the van up the dirt road, and away from what was left of El Rancho, she began to shake—first a quiver in her shoulders and then down her arms to her knees, building momentum as it spread. She pulled the van over to the side of the road.

Maggie needed to gather herself until she got out of this godforsaken land. *Cry later,* she told herself. Yes, cry when you are safely back in the USA.

Maya—who had turned down Maggie's offer to join her, "I am going to Argentina to live with a cousin and start my life over"—had given her directions to the border crossing. It was simple enough, except that she had to drive through the village where many of the field hands lived. She and Chick had driven through it on the way, and she had hardly given it a notice—a little hardscrabble nothing place of ramshackle buildings made of wood and adobe.

She shifted into first gear and accelerated, trying to concentrate on the road ahead, and not the nightmarish events of last night.

Approaching the village, Maggie had to fight her nerves as her hands began to shake. "Stop it," she told herself as she slowed the car. "Drive yourself carefully through and out of here." The place was quiet, and only a few people were about, women mostly; one was sweeping the porch of a store, another cleaning the windows of what looked like a trinket shop.

As Maggie was about to exit the village, two men appeared, walking toward her on the side of the road. They were short brown men dressed in denim shirts and jeans. Field hands! They seemed tired but pleased, as though good fortune had come their way.

The sight of them sent a shudder of fear through Maggie, as she saw them catch her eye as she passed. In that moment their expressions changed to that of disgraced fear: the mouths slightly agape, the eyes saying, *Forgive us.*

At the border crossing into Arizona, Maggie was asked to pull over. A large German shepherd sniffed around and inside the van. Another US Customs officer approached Maggie, who was standing off to the side trying to control her shaking knees. "Where you headed, miss?"

"California," Maggie said, forcing a smile. "Good to be back in the USA," she said with a confirming nod.

"Hmm," the policeman said as he eyed Maggie and then the van suspiciously. "Funky-looking vehicle you got there."

The officer with the dog said the van was clean.

The suspicious cop kept his gaze on Maggie, who stood there trying her damndest to show she hadn't a care in the world. But on the inside, she was screaming silent howls of anguish, not just for this going-over she was receiving but for all that had transpired.

"Okay," the suspicious cop said to Maggie, "you're good to go."

A few miles past the border, Maggie stopped at a diner, not only to eat, but to figure out a where she was going. The carnage and destruction from yesterday were put on the back burner as she felt a compelling instinctive urge to get far away from El Rancho. She must keep it together.

Before departing El Rancho, she had dressed in jeans and a solid gray sweatshirt, of Chick's, stored in the back of the van, wanting to look as plain and simple as possible. Then she checked every part of the van for drugs: under and behind the seats, the glove compartment, under the hood, and even scrunching down on her back underneath the belly of the car. The only thing she found was an envelope under the front seat with the keys. Inside were five one-hundred-dollar bills and a note:

Maggie,

You will not see me again. If I make it across, I am heading off on my own. It's best for you that I am out of your life.

Chick

Maggie had a sense that Chick had thought he was doomed. Even if he made it across safely, there was a part of him that saw the flaw: the need for risk and danger. She remembered in high school, Chick telling her that the bigger and more dangerous a wave, the more he wanted to not only surf it but to challenge it. And he took that mind-set in his drug dealings. Why else would he have gone into the Mexican badlands when he knew the dangers? Maggie wondered if, in a part of Chick, there hadn't been a death wish.

She felt bad for Chick's demise, but if it hadn't been here, it would have been somewhere else. *Whatever will be will be.*

Chick's money added to a grand total of a little over ten thousand in cash, plus a few thousand back home in a savings account. Enough to keep her head above water for a good while, but with the baby due in five months, she needed a plan.

She ordered her food and looked out the window; the Arizona landscape was starkly beautiful: scrubby landscape of cactus and tumbleweed, in the distance the outline of mountains backdropped by a faint blue sky. How beautiful yet so lonely.

For a moment Maggie thought about returning to Bethesda and letting Johnny know he was going to be a father, but too much had passed. Maggie had changed. The horror at the ranch was etched in her mind, and going back home seemed like regression. She was not who she used to be. Whether that was for the good or not, only time would tell.

Going west appealed to her, but where? Not Manhassa Beach, no place to raise a kid. Up to Northern California, where she had gone to college, again no. She needed somewhere that wasn't too expensive, where she could raise a child and find a job, and find exactly what it was she wanted to do. A degree in English literature wasn't much help. What did appeal to her was something to do with preparing and cooking food.

While at the ranch, Maggie had learned many things from Maya about Mexican cuisine: how to dry, shell, and grind corn for heavenly tortillas, a slew of delicious yet simple recipes such as an out-of-this-world spicy chicken soup, and, also, Maya was an efficient, no time wasted cook. Toward the end, Maggie was nearly on Maya's level in the kitchen. "You are natural-born cook," Maya had told her more than once.

Maggie could start off as a waitress and work her way into the kitchen, but it must be in a place that provided a safe environment for her and her child.

So where to go? Maggie thought as she drove west. She remembered the last lines in the famous poem "The Road Not Taken," by Robert Frost, a line of which Johnny had paraphrased in his drawing of her: "The girl who takes the road less traveled."

> Two roads diverge in a wood, and I—
> I took the one less traveled by,
> And that has made all the difference.

Maggie got onto Interstate 8 and soon she was driving across the Sonoran Desert. There was little traffic, and the scenery had that same beautiful yet lonely feel as back at the diner. It seemed to fit Maggie, beautiful yet lonely. She didn't feel lonely exactly, more just alone. And that didn't seem such a bad thing at this stage. Since she was thirteen, boys had been in and out of her life. They were drawn to not only her looks but that pull-them-in personality.

Maggie did enjoy the company of men, not just the romance. Back in Bethesda working at the Raw Bar, Maggie looked forward every Friday evening for Johnny and his buddies to come into the back room and swallow the place up with their loud jokes and big-guy personalities. And she gave it back to them as good as they gave it and then some. And they loved her for it and she them. They were her kind of guys: big athletic guys, shot-and-a-beer kind of guys who enjoyed a good laugh at each other's expense, guys who were comfortable in their own skin. She imagined she would never experience anything like the camaraderie she felt with her boys from Bethesda. But it was time to turn the page.

Crossing into California, the dry, arid landscape changed little. But a couple of hours later, the topography began to change to rolling hills, with small towns and farms here and there. And off in the distance, to the north, was a line of green hills. Something about those hills seemed appealing. What it was, Maggie wasn't sure, but soon she would find out.

CHAPTER 18

The sign up ahead read Los Angeles 100 Miles. That was close enough. Maggie took the next exit and headed north onto a two-lane highway. She was in farmland, small-town America that most people did not relate to California.

Farther on, the land became greener and with more trees. At a crossroad, an overhead sign indicated an interstate to her right, to her left the Village of Empire Springs. Robert Frost's closing line waffled in her mind like a warm spring breeze, encouraging Maggie to turn left, to take the road less traveled.

The road meandered through farmland and woodland with conifer trees and woody plants. The woodland floor had a covering of pine needles and pine cones. There was something reassuring about this gentle land, the green hills now closing in as though welcoming her to proceed.

Around a bend, the village came into view. Maggie knew immediately that the left turn she had taken was the right one: The Village of Empire Springs was two blocks of pure old-town charm. The town hall was an A-frame timber structure with a wraparound front porch; beautiful it was. There was a country store with a couple of old boys sitting in rocking chairs, who offered a wave to Maggie, who waved back. Past a line of small shops and businesses, at the end of the village, was a large red brick building, with three front doors and stoops, with a sign out front for available office space. Farther down, past the town proper, was a tree-lined street, the beginning of a neighborhood of white picket fences and sturdy wood-framed homes.

To Maggie's right, across the street from the office building, was the post office. Its exterior of board-and-batten siding drew Maggie's eye. Next to the post office was a clapboard two-story building that looked to have been a house at one time, with a fresh coat of white paint and a sign on the plate-glass window, Millie's Place.

Maggie parked in a gravel parking lot between the post office and the restaurant, the crunch of tires on gravel registering in little shock waves tingling down her spine. It came over her that she was tired, very tired. She had not slept in two days and was running on adrenaline.

Millie's Place was along the lines of a well-maintained country restaurant. There were booths along a wall, a stone fireplace to the right of the front door, past which a staircase led to a landing, and occupying the heart of the room were round oak tables that seated four with ladder-back chairs, except a large table in the middle with seven chairs. Ensconced in a nook in a back corner was a horseshoe bar.

It was early evening, and Maggie had not eaten since morning. Most of the tables were occupied with folks anywhere from late twenties to sixties. One couple in a booth, who looked to be in their early fifties, studied Maggie for a moment, the woman offering a welcoming smile.

Maggie was standing off to the side of the front door when a rosy-cheeked woman with a shock of prematurely white hair, which she wore in a short, no-nonsense pageboy, approached.

"Sit anywhere you like, hon," the woman said. She had light blue eyes that seemed to transmit a certain hospitable warmth, but behind the warmth there was strength of one who had endured a difficult time in her life. Maggie figured this was Millie; she looked like a Millie: average height, stocky but not fat, and a bit of the tomboy about her as though she had been an athlete in her day.

Maggie smiled a thank-you and took a seat in a booth. She took a closer look at the place, and everything she saw she liked. She wasn't certain what the hardwood flooring was, maybe redwood? It was reddish-brown with a slightly coarse texture that gave the space a back-in-the-day look, as did the bead-board ceiling with two paddle fans.

Maggie turned to the *whoosh* of the double kitchen doors opening.

A teenage boy emerged with a platter of food and took it to the couple in their fifties, who were sitting in the booth in front of Maggie. "Steak just the way you like, Mr. O'Connor," the boy said, "blood rare."

Mr. O'Connor gave a thumbs-up and winked his approval. Even in his fifties, this man maintained a youthful look about him. He had a rippled thicket of mahogany-gray hair, broad shoulders, and a strong chin. There was a trace of loose flesh in the neck, but the face was remarkably unlined, and there was an overlay of education in his manner. He had an elegant yet rough-hewn aura about him, this man, Mr. O'Connor, who appeared the type of fellow who could still draw a woman's eye of admiration. "Thank you, Daniel," Mr. O'Connor said in a strong voice; it was a voice of power, a voice of success.

Daniel served the woman, saying in a respectful voice, "Mrs. O'Connor." She turned to Daniel and offered another of her patented smiles: the lips opened wide to reveal a row of strong white teeth. Mrs. O'Connor wore little if any makeup, and her skin had a honey-brown glow indicating vigorous exercise and good health. Even at their age, they were the best-looking couple in the room: the homecoming queen and the star athlete in their golden years.

The diners were dressed in corduroy and flannel, sweaters and jeans, and only a couple of the women were wearing dresses. Maggie was wearing shorts, T-shirt, and sandals, which she had changed into at the diner in Arizona, and though she didn't feel underdressed, she felt a bit of a chill as the temperature outside was in the sixties. After four months of the heat in Mexico, this was a nice relief.

The boy came to the table and put down a water and menu. "Meatloaf is the special tonight," he said. "My mom," he said with a lift of his chin in the direction of Millie taking an order at another table, "made it." He was about fifteen, and it struck Maggie that he was similar in age to Eduardo. Poor Maya, no son or uncle left. It surprised Maggie how resilient that salt-of-the-earth woman was. She took the death of her son and uncle with a sort of calm remorse, her dark eyes crying silent tears.

Maggie tried to read the menu, but her eyes would not focus. She leaned back in the booth and took a deep breath. It was amazing to think that just yesterday, she was nearly raped and murdered, and now she was sitting in a country restaurant in the middle of California, trying to figure out the rest of her life. She had been on the road for over ten hours, and a wave of fatigue came over her.

She felt a sudden chill as her eyes swelled with tears. Maggie began sobbing, first in little gurgles of grief and then a tidal wave.

Heads were turning to see what the commotion was about. Maggie tried to stifle her sobs, but it was no use. It was as though a relief valve had been turned on. She buried her face in her hands.

Maggie felt a hand on her shoulder. "Hon, you all right?" Maggie looked up as Millie offered her a Kleenex.

Maggie tried to speak, but she could not get the words out through the gasping sobs. Millie slid into the booth next to Maggie, wrapped an arm around her shoulder and said, "Let it all out, hon, let it all out."

Maggie felt an immediate calm from the warm embrace. "Sorry," Maggie murmured as she gathered herself. She wiped her eyes with the Kleenex and drew in a deep breath.

"How about some food," Millie said more as a statement.

"Thank you," Maggie said. "Thank you."

Millie served Maggie a steaming bowl of chicken soup, followed by ham and cheese on rye with a tossed salad with a sweet-and-sour vinaigrette dressing. Maggie ate every bit of it.

After Daniel cleared Maggie's table, Millie sat across from her in the booth.

"Looks like you enjoyed my cooking," Millie said. "By the way, I'm Millie Kendricks."

"I'm Maggie Meyers."

"Aren't you though," Millie said with a grin and a nod.

"Your food was very good," Maggie said as she glanced around as the last of the customers departed. "Did you grow up here?"

"Marvelous place to grow up and raise a child." Millie peered at Maggie for a moment as if trying to see if she were catching her drift. "This was a big lumberjack town back in the day, but not so much anymore."

Millie's voice had a calming effect on Maggie. It was strong yet unforced as though they had been friends for years. "My dad was a lumberjack as were both my grandfathers."

Millie went on to tell Maggie that her husband had died two months after Daniel was conceived. "It was tough, but I had the child to think about," she said with a knowing lift of the brow. "Not sure what you're going through," Millie added, "and I don't need to know."

Maggie asked if she needed help. "I've waited tables and can cook some, especially Mexican."

Lord, yes, hon," Millie said, "I lost my cook-dishwasher last week and have been running around here like a chicken with my head cut off." Millie leaned forward, eyes opened in an exaggerated manner, and a how-do-you-like-that expression. Maggie burst out laughing, and Millie followed suit. And in their laughter a bond began to form, two women drawn together: one in need of help, the other in need of helping. "Hon," Millie said through a face-splitting grin, "I believe this is the beginning of a good, long friendship."

CHAPTER 19

I t was two in the afternoon, and Maggie was resting upstairs on a sofa in Millie's office. Daniel had to study for a biology exam, and so it would be just Maggie, Millie, and the new guy, Raymond.

It had been three months since Maggie arrived, and the baby was due in seven weeks. She was staying temporally at Millie's house. "You can stay in the guest room at my house until you get things sorted out, hon," Millie had told her the first night in town.

After a couple days in Empire Springs, Maggie told Millie her complete story, from Johnny O'Brien and his heart condition to Chick and Mexico, murders and all. It felt good to unload this story on Millie. It was during the lull between lunch and dinner, and they were sitting on the back porch of the restaurant. Millie just sat there and listened, and when Maggie had finished, she took hold of Maggie's hand and said, "You're in a good place now, hon."

And so right Millie was, and to top it off, the pregnancy had gone smoothly. Millie had taken Maggie for a checkup to Dr. Robert Alderson, but everyone called him Rack, a local boy who had graduated from UCLA Medical School and returned to his home roots. He was married with two teenage children, boy and girl, and lived and practiced on four acres of land a couple of miles north of town.

Rack had warned Maggie about abstaining from alcohol and drug use. Not that he was normally opposed to either: Millie told Maggie that he had a marijuana garden in the middle of his vineyard.

Maggie had been abstaining since her first inkling that she was pregnant.

Another thing she had been abstinent from was sex. She had a couple of offers for dates from some blue-collar guys in their thirties, who worked for O'Connor Construction and Home Building Co. and drank a few cold ones at the bar after work from time to time.

But this was a small town, and when the inevitable time came to break it off, Maggie would see the guy around, and she might well be looked down upon by the town folk.

Maggie swung her legs off the sofa and stood. She stretched her arms over her head. These naps, which Millie had insisted on, were a lifesaver. "I took a nap every afternoon for the last four months carrying Daniel, and you'll need to do the same," Millie had said to Maggie her first day on the job, seeming to have surmised Maggie's pregnancy, though, at the time, she had been showing very little in clothes.

Maggie went into the bathroom across the hall from the office. She looked into the mirror. Her cheeks glowed, contrasting beautifully with her creamy olive skin. She felt a kick and placed her hand on her belly. "Hello down there," she said.

She splashed water on her face and reached for a washcloth on the rack. While her body was swelling in not only the stomach but her hips, her face appeared the same: the finely structured cheekbones; full lips, lips that could twist and turn to indicate a change in mood. Johnny once told her, "Not only are your lips devastatingly beautiful, but they are like a barometer to your moods."

She dried her face with the cloth and leaned into the mirror looking into her eyes. Eyes that Johnny had told her were like portholes into her soul. He used to call her "my brown-eyed girl." She could almost hear Johnny's voice whispering in her ear.

The clanging of pots downstairs broke the moment and alerted Maggie that Millie was down in the kitchen beginning the dinner menu. She had taken Maggie under her wing, the mother bear looking after a stray cub that roamed into her territory. Maggie waited tables mostly, and she got more than a few ogles from the men, young and old, even now wearing Millie's old maternity shirts.

Maggie got dressed and found Millie in the kitchen scrubbing potatoes in the sink. "What can I do?" Maggie asked.

"Good rest, Maggie?" Millie said.

"I'm good," Maggie said as she moved toward a bushel basket packed with vegetables from Millie's garden. "What's going into the beef stew for tonight?"

"How about you decide."

"Really?" Maggie said as though not quite believing.

"Chuck roast in fridge, bay leaves … oh," Millie said with a wave of her hand, "you know where everything is."

"I'd like to try something a little different," Maggie said as she bent down and removed a bunch of carrots from the basket. She slid a look over at Millie.

"Just remember," Millie said, "our customers—"

"Are simple folks with simple tastes," Maggie cut in with a knowing smile and a nod toward her boss.

The back door of the kitchen opened, and Raymond entered. He was a big, shaggy guy, early forties, graying hair in a ponytail, who had the look of one who had allowed the sixties to get the better of him. "Ladies," Raymond said as he lifted the bushel basket up on the counter. "What's the deal this evening, Millie?"

"Daniel has to study for an exam." Millie shot Raymond a bemused look that said, "You know what's coming."

"Ah," Raymond said raising his hands and pretending to inspect them. "I be the sous-chef, bottle washer, busboy, *and* whatever else the madam of the house may *require*." He said the word "require" with a special twist as though he were putting a spin on a ball.

Millie tilted her head back and faked laughing. "You be so right, Ray … monn."

Raymond took an apron off a hook and said, "I do love it so when we banter about misconjugated verbs." He slipped on the apron and offered a mock bow toward Millie. "Touché."

By three, Maggie had braised the bone-in roast and then cubed the meat and left the bone in the pot for additional flavor, diced the carrots/celery/potatoes, cut long slices of Vidalia onions, and went out back and pulled a couple of cobs of corn from the garden and stripped the kernels. All this was similar to Millie's recipe. She then added her Mexican influence: mild green chilies that she diced very fine, garlic, chili powder, cumin, and dried oregano. She was careful to cut back on the proportions, but wanted to added some zest and spice to the dish.

Meanwhile, Raymond was setting the tables and helping Wilbur stock the bar. Wilbur had run a sawmill on his property for thirty years before he turned the operation over to his son. His wife was a good friend of Millie, and when the former bartender left, Wilbur came on board a few years back. He was a bearded good old boy, bald, and with personality that was perfect for tending bar: attentive to detail, an even-keel sort of fellow who could tell a joke and laugh at one. And to top it off, he was built like a beer keg, with a barrel chest and thick arms. He had the look of a man who was not unfamiliar with hard work.

Millie sliced iceberg lettuce, also from the garden, and diced some vegetables, including fat beefeater tomatoes, and then mixed the contents in plastic bags and stored them in the fridge.

The menu at Millie's Place, which served lunch and dinner, was basic: one dinner special each night plus steaks, fried chicken, burgers and sandwiches, steamed vegetables, coleslaw, baked or fried potatoes, and a few simple appetizers such as chicken wings. This made it easier to run the restaurant efficiently with a small staff, and Millie was ruthlessly efficient and then some. She wasted nothing, such as saving trimmed fat, using it later on the griddle to add an additional flavor. And she could be cooking away in the kitchen and then check on the dining area and bar, meet and greet folks, and give an order or two that she always did in a respectful manner but with a tone that said, "I am in charge." And then she was back in the kitchen in time to flip burgers or pull a batch of fries.

Maggie had learned a lot from Millie, not only about how to run a business, but how to raise a child without a man in her life. Daniel was a great kid, who never complained about any of his duties, from emptying the trash, busing, helping in the kitchen when needed, and, what he enjoyed most, waiting tables.

Millie allowed Daniel some leeway in how he dressed. "Jeans and sneakers okay, but must wear a shirt with a collar." She also was sensitive to his schoolwork, though the boy loved to work at his mother's restaurant, seeming to feed off the energy of not only the customers but his mother, who he called *Mom* in front of everyone. Daniel was always polite and never got upset when customers complained. "The customer is always right," he would say with a shrug upon returning a dish to the kitchen.

Mother and son interacted more as partners, though uneven for sure, for Millie always had the last word. Of course, it seemed, Millie always had the last word. She seemed to be a step ahead of what a customer might need or was about to say.

Millie had told Maggie that Daniel was his father's son. "Big Dan never complained a day in his life," Millie told her one evening after hours as they sat at the bar, Millie with a glass of Cabernet and Maggie soda water and lime.

Dan Kendricks and Millie had known each other all their lives, growing up together in Empire Springs, and married after Dan graduated college with a degree in forestry. He took a job working for the Park Service as a ranger. Millie didn't go to college. "Dan and I planned to marry after he got his degree, and I went to work for O'Connor Construction as a secretary to save money for the home we eventually built."

Millie dug into her purse and showed Maggie a picture of her husband in his ranger uniform. He was a tall, lanky man with short-cropped dark hair and a lean, friendly face. Maggie saw some of Daniel in his father, the long body, but also Millie in the boy's fair skin and the light blue eyes. "He's all Big Dan in demeanor," Millie said with a remembering smile. She took a sip of her wine and smiled again, this time tinged with regret. "They would have been great together," Millie added, "but it was not meant to be."

The pot roast was not only a big hit. Mr. and Mrs. O'Connor split a second bowl, and another table raved to Maggie about it: "Delicious," a woman commented. Her husband piped in, "Damn fine pot roast, Maggie." The prepared dinner special made it easy for Maggie to wait on tables and help in the kitchen. All she had to do was ladle out a portion in a bowl and serve.

Maggie felt as though she might have found a home in Empire Springs; not only were most of the customers and folks in town friendly, there wasn't one cross-eyed look at this young newcomer, single and pregnant. Maggie received nothing but support: "When's the baby due?" or "Do you want a boy or a girl?"

Angie McCrowley, the town librarian, who enjoyed nursing a sherry at the bar after work, always had a kind word for Maggie. Angie was in her forties, single, rail thin, with mouse-brown hair in a neat little bun, and she wore wire-rim glasses that she would peer over to make a cogent point. She looked and dressed—long skirt and white blouse with frilly collar buttoned at the top—like a librarian, but with a quiet spirit about her as though she were comfortable with whom she was and the seemingly solitary life she lived. And just a couple of days ago, Angie said to Maggie, "There's nothing more precious on God's green earth than a newborn. You'll make a wonderful mother, Maggie, you surely will."

One woman at the pharmacy asked Maggie if she had picked out names yet. Maggie replied, "If it's a boy, John. Not sure about a girl's name."

"Is your husband named John?"

"It's the father's name," Maggie said without a trace of guilt.

"Oh," the woman said. She then nodded and forced a smile. "It is a fine name." And that was about as bad as it got for Maggie in regard to her marital status or lack thereof.

CHAPTER 20

Maggie woke as she felt a stirring down in her privates. She sat up in bed as she discharged a gush of water. "Millie," Maggie called out. The creak of bedsprings in the next room followed by the pad of footsteps, and then the hallway lights snapped on. "Is it time, hon?" Millie said as she entered the bedroom.

Both women turned to the window at the *whoosh* of wind and the pelting *rat-a-tat-tat-tat* of sleety rain against the glass. "Don't want to try and drive these old country roads at night, all the way to the hospital in this weather," Millie said.

They exchanged looks and then Millie said, "Let me call Rack." She went out in the hallway. "Sorry to wake the house, Carey," Millie said. "Is Rack there?"

There was silence, and then Millie said, "As soon as he returns, have him call my house."

Millie explained to Maggie, "There's been an auto accident. Rack's gone to the hospital."

Maggie asked if they shouldn't drive there.

"Hon," Millie said in her even-as-you-go tone, "this is your first pregnancy. It's gonna take a good long while." She put her hand on Maggie's forehead. "How do you feel, Maggie?"

Three hours into the labor, Maggie groaned something fierce as she felt a sharp pain in her lower back and abdomen.

The phone rang, and Millie answered it.

"Rack is on the way," Millie said from the doorway. "I just have to get a few things for him."

"Oh," Maggie gasped as a burning sensation gripped her chest and shot down her legs. It seemed as if her body was going to rip apart. She felt a strong contraction move in waves like menstrual cramps, but stronger—much stronger. Maggie thought she might pass out from the pain. "Millie! I think … the baby … is coming," Maggie screamed through hurried breath.

Millie came back into the room with two clean towels, and with some effort she rolled Maggie on her side, and back onto the towels. "I need to wash up; be right back, hon."

Maggie screamed and howled as the contractions were arriving like tidal waves, her uterus seemingly ready to explode.

Millie returned and lifted Maggie's nightgown and then slid off her underwear. "Take my hand, Maggie," Millie said. "Breathe easy, hon." Even in her excruciating pain, the warmth and confidence of Millie's touch let Maggie know she was in good hands.

"Bring your knees up and push hard, Maggie," Millie said as she reached down with both hands, as Maggie felt the baby coming out. She looked down and saw Millie holding a head with a tangle of wet dark hair. Maggie pushed hard as she grunted out her breaths. Soon a pair of shoulders emerged and then the baby. *It's a boy!*

The hurried clop of footsteps caused both women to look toward the door as Rack came into the room with medical bag in hand. "Millie, clean towel, and a couple of dry washcloths." Rack turned his attention to the new mother. "I'll wash up and be right there, Maggie."

Rack sat on the side of the bed next to Maggie, examining the baby, still attached to the umbilical cord. He reached into his bag, removed what he needed from a plastic bag, secured two clamps on the cord, and then cut in between with scissors.

Millie returned and handed Rack a washcloth that he wiped the baby down with. He then placed the baby boy on Maggie's stomach and put the towel over the child.

Rack then wiped Maggie's damp forehead; she hadn't even noticed how wet she was. "That's one fine-looking baby boy, Maggie," Rack said with a reassuring nod.

Maggie slid her hands underneath the towel on the baby's back; its little warm body offered her a comfort and sense of well-being she never imagined existed. This was her child, her baby boy.

"Well," Rack said, "got a name for the handsome fella?"

"John," Maggie said with a lift in her voice, "John O'Brien."

CHAPTER 21

Millie insisted that Maggie not work for the first two months after John was born. "We can handle the restaurant," she told her a few days after the birth. "You look after the baby, and I'll look after work. It'll still be there when you return." Part of Maggie wanted to argue, but the maternal side ruled out. "You're a godsend, Millie."

They were in Millie's kitchen, Maggie breastfeeding at the kitchen table and Millie at the stove preparing breakfast. Millie's timber A-frame house, much like the restaurant, had a down-home charm to it, with a country kitchen of pine and salvaged timber. Off the kitchen was the spacious living room: stone fireplace, ship's table, refurbished chest, long comfy sofa upholstered in napped cotton, matching chairs. Two paintings: one an overhead of Main Street in town, including Millie's Place; the other, a sawmill along a river. That was most of the house, other than Daniel's bedroom off the hallway and the upstairs with three bedrooms, one of which Millie used to store odds and ends. There was a full bath upstairs and down.

At the pad of footsteps from the hallway, Maggie covered the back of the baby's head with a towel to shield her exposed breast.

"Morning," Daniel said as he placed his book bag on the table. "Running late for varsity club meeting, Mom."

Millie handed him a scrambled egg sandwich wrapped in a napkin. "Drink some juice before you go."

Daniel poured a glass from a pitcher of orange juice on the table and downed it. "Ahhh," he said through an exaggerated smile. "Off to school and then basketball practice, and then the dinner shift at the restaurant." He slung his book bag over his shoulder and started to make his way out, when he stopped and looked over his shoulder at his mother, a bemused smile creasing the corner of his mouth. "Aren't there child labor laws around these parts?"

Millie leaned her head back, brow raised.

"Just kidding, Mom," Daniel said. He shot a smile at Maggie. "Some day she will figure out when I'm kidding."

He pivoted around at the honk of a car horn, his long legs in full stride at the first step, taking him through the hallway and out the front door.

When John was finished breastfeeding, Maggie put him in a basinet, buttoned back up her blouse, and lifted John up to her shoulder, patting his back. John let out a loud burp. It always amazed her that such a small body could emit such a sound. Maggie then placed him back in the basinet as Millie served breakfast.

Maggie asked how things were going at the restaurant, still a tad guilty about not helping out.

Millie slathered an English muffin with a pat of butter and took a thoughtful bite. "Everything's running fine, especially this time of year; with the rain and all, business slows some."

"I don't know where John and I would be without you, Millie," Maggie said with meaning, as a twitch of emotion rose in her throat.

Millie leaned over and placed the back of her hand on John's cheek for a moment and then took hold of Maggie's wrist. "I'd like you and John to move into the house permanently with me and Daniel."

"Millie—"

Millie raised her hand to indicate she wasn't done talking. "Raising a baby alone is not the way to go."

Maggie placed her scrambled egg atop her muffin and cut it into four sections. "I accept," Maggie said as she raised a forkful of food toward her mouth and stopped. "But you must allow me to pay rent." Maggie began eating and at the same time made a face—*okay?*

"Deal," Millie said. She raised a finger to indicate one more thing. "And when John is old enough, he can have the spare bedroom upstairs."

After Millie left for work, Maggie took John upstairs into her now-permanent bedroom and changed his diaper on the bed. Maggie had to admit, he was a beautiful baby. He had a head of black downy silk for hair, the eyebrows perfectly formed, and perfect symmetry of his button nose and dark blue eyes—innocent eyes that were watching his mother with a look of wonder. He was his father's son.

Maggie tucked John into his crib, like the basinet, Daniel's hand-me-down, and went out into the hall and picked up the phone.

"Maggie," Nora said in a tone of relieved surprise.

Maggie told Nora neither about Mexico nor the baby but instead said only that she was working at a restaurant in a small town in Central California. "But I would like you to keep it to yourself, Nora."

"Not a problem, Maggie."

"How's Johnny?"

"We didn't see him at the Raw Bar for almost a month after you left."

Nora went on to say that Johnny's mother had been struck by a car in Bethesda and had died.

"Oh no," Maggie said as a fleeting thought whisked in her head. *What if I had stayed, would marriage …?* "How did Johnny handle it?" Maggie said.

"Okay," Nora said in a careful tone. "After the funeral, we all went to the Knights. Everyone was there, and Johnny's spirits picked up as he went from table to table sharing memories."

Part of Maggie wished she had been there, to be at Johnny's side and in the company of his boys. She did miss all of them. But now that seemed like another life.

They talked about the Raw Bar. "Nothing has changed," Nora said. "Same old guys at the bar. Johnny and his crew still come in on Friday nights after basketball." Nora also mentioned that Tip and Danny had moved into Johnny's mother's house with him. "He remodeled the basement into a bar and hung a carved wooden sign over it—The Bethesdan."

"Is Johnny dating anyone?"

"Seen him at two parties, each time with a different girl, nothing serious," Nora said.

Maggie gave Nora the addresses to the restaurant and Millie's house, and the phone numbers. Nora was not the chatty type, and Maggie doubted she would call very often, but she wanted her to have contact information in case something was to happen to Johnny.

And she knew that it wasn't fair to not let Johnny know he had a son. But something deep in Maggie's core told her to hold up. She did not want to go back east and live, and Johnny would be lost out here away from his friends and his beloved Bethesda. And what would she tell her son as the years went by about his father? And what if he inherited his father's heart condition? She knew she had to let Rack know about it, but, *I have some time to figure all that out,* she thought as she checked on the baby in the crib. He was still awake, his alert eyes watching Maggie. She lifted John up and held him cheek to cheek. How lovely he smelled of talc and that clean baby smell. The smell of innocence and youth. Maggie never thought she could love anyone more than Johnny O'Brien, but their son had taken it to a new level.

Maggie brought the baby in front of her face and said, "You'll never turn me down, will you …" She paused and kissed John on both cheeks and said, "Will you, *son?*"

CHAPTER 22

"I know just the right woman for day care," Millie told Maggie a couple of weeks before she was to return to work.

It was a lazy Sunday morning in the living room, the only day the restaurant was closed, Maggie and Millie in their nightgowns, lounging on the sofa reading the local Sunday paper, John sound asleep in the basinet.

"Oh," Maggie said as she looked up from reading *Prince Valiant*—Val got drunk celebrating the birth of his first son, Prince Nathan. She had always thought Johnny a perfect Prince Valiant.

Millie went on to say that the woman lived less than ten minutes away, "Just the other side of town from here." And Millie had Maggie and John's schedule worked out. "Two days a week you pick him up at day care after the lunch rush and then head home." Maggie put the comics aside and started to say something, but Millie raised her hand. "The first year, it's important for a mother to spend one-on-one time with her child," she said. "Then the other days, you pick him up before the dinner rush and bring him back to the restaurant and set him up in my office."

Millie raised her finger as if to say one more thing. She went to the refurbished chest next to the fireplace. She removed a box wrapped in light brown gift paper with a blue ribbon bow.

Maggie carefully removed the ribbon and paper. The Nursery Monitor box had two pictures, one of a baby sleeping in a crib, monitor attached to the wall, and the other a smiling mother in the kitchen with a monitor on the counter. Below the pictures was, "Let's you be in two places at once."

"We'll set up the other monitor in the kitchen." Millie made a face— *What do you think?*

"Two places at once," Maggie said through an appreciative smile. "It's perfect, Millie, perfect."

The days off after lunch allowed Maggie to schedule her postnatal exams with Rack and not have to ask for time off from work. And over the course of time, something passed between the doctor and Maggie. At first it was all business discussing the baby's health, which was "very healthy," to a lingering look of admiration that progressed to a hand on the shoulder and tap of the wrist.

Rack had curly brown hair and deeply set eyes with a gaze of a certain profundity—he would have been a perfect typecast for a doctor on a soap opera—but along with it came a bohemian bent with his penchant for growing his own dope and making homemade wine.

Rack had never mentioned his marijuana garden to Maggie, and even if he did, she didn't know where or when she could find the time. If she wasn't with the baby, she was working.

It was late afternoon, and Maggie was waiting in Rack's reception area. His office was a converted three-car garage and was connected to the house by a breezeway. Rack lived in a refurbished farmhouse that he and his wife, Carey, had bought a few years after he started his practice.

The doctor came into the reception area. "Maggie," Rack said, in a tone of seeing an old chum. He turned to his nurse, an older white-haired woman. "Martha, why don't you head on home? I'll take it from here."

Rack examined John from head to toe, stethoscope for heartbeat, and so on. He then went over the upcoming series of shots the baby would receive. By the end of the discussion, John had fallen asleep in the basinet. Rack looked over at the child and turned his gaze on Maggie. "You like weed?"

"Thought you'd never ask." Maggie raised her brow as if to say the ball is in your court.

Rack dug into his pocket and pulled out a fat doobie, a beautiful doobie. "Let's go to my outdoor conference area." He motioned to a sliding glass door that opened to a brick patio.

They kept the door open and sat in Adirondack chairs, with a view of the vineyard, which was no more than two acres. From this vantage point, Maggie could see the top leaves of marijuana plants in the middle. Unless one was specifically looking, these would be hard to spot. Past the vineyard was the line of green mountains that had originally drawn her toward Empire Springs. Above the mountains was an orange sun that sat high and strong in the western sky.

Rack handed the doobie to Maggie. "You may have the honor of the first pull." He struck a match and Maggie drew deeply. She held the smoke for a moment and exhaled.

"Been a while, has it?" Rack said as he took the joint and held it for a moment, eyes dancing with mischief.

They took three drags apiece before Maggie said she was good.

Rack snuffed out the doobie and stored it back into his pocket. They were sitting next to each other. Rack reached over and put his hand on Maggie's. She turned and looked at him and in that moment realized she had a decision to make.

CHAPTER 23

By the time John was eighteen months old, Maggie and her son's life in Empire Springs was good if somewhat predictable.

One thing that wasn't predictable was Maggie and Rack sharing a joint on his patio. These sessions were few and far between, sometimes months, when both had a pocket of free time. And Rack's advance to take it further, their first time, had been met by Maggie telling him, "No, Rack. We can't go there."

Rack had nodded as if he understood and then said, "I understand, small town, married doc, single mother in town."

"Exactly," Maggie replied.

So Maggie kept it on a platonic level with Rack, sharing a joint on his patio every now and then. And Maggie looked forward to it. Rack was smart, and funny in an offbeat sort of way with a variety of epigrams: "Can't cope ... don't mope," Rack said through a Cheshire cat grin. "There's hope ... smoke dope."

After their last time sharing a joint, Rack asked, in his casual breezy way, who or what Maggie was running from. "A pregnant woman doesn't show up in Empire Springs unless something or someone drove her away, or," he said as he looked at Maggie, searching for a reaction, "a combination of the two."

Rack seemed good at keeping secrets, but even more so he was someone who would not pass judgment.

"John's father was the love of my life, and he wouldn't marry me because of an incurable heart condition." Maggie went on about her courtship and rejection, the trip to Mexico with Chick and the murders.

"Wow," Rack said with a trace of awe in his voice. "That would make a hell of a story."

"Here's the thing, Rack," Maggie said as she took a deep toke and exhaled. "There's a chance John has inherited his father's heart condition." She handed the joint to Rack who held it, a question in his eyes.

"What's the name of it?"

"Hypertrophic …"

"Hypertrophic cardiomyopathy," Rack said. He took a quick pull on the joint and gazed out at the vineyard for a moment before turning his attention back to Maggie. "I have a friend from med school who is a pediatric heart specialist in Los Angeles. I'll arranged an appointment and drive you and John."

Two weeks later, on Wednesday morning, Maggie arrived with John at Rack's house. She found the office door locked and went to the front door of the residence and rang the doorbell.

Carey answered the door. Maggie had waited on her with Rack and their two children and with her tennis-playing girlfriends at Millie's Place. Millie called them "snooty girls who think they are too good for Empire Springs."

Rack's wife was tall and lean with short brown hair and jade-green eyes. Rack had told Maggie that Carey had been a member of the tennis team in college. "She hated to lose," Rack had said. And to Maggie that partly explained her inclination to look severe in unguarded moments. Carey was never overtly rude to Maggie when she waited on her, nor were her tennis chums, but they had an attitude of superiority.

"Hello there," Carey said. "Maggie, isn't it?"

Maggie was holding John in her arms. "Yes." She was going to say how much she appreciated her husband taking the time for her and her son but held back upon the probing once-over she was receiving. It was an arched brow look of appraisal, a look of suspicion.

Carey stepped back and motioned Maggie into the foyer. This was Maggie's first time inside the house, and the interior was not what she had expected for a farmhouse. At the end of the foyer was the dining room with an intricately woven carpet, a gaudy chandelier hanging over a shiny mahogany table supported by thin fluted legs, stiff high-back chairs around the long table, and ornate crown molding. The living room was more of the same with a couple of gilt-framed paintings, uncomfortable-looking high-back chairs and a stiff-as-a board sofa at the back of the room. The décor matched this woman standing before Maggie. And the furnishing and the woman belonged in a New York penthouse, not Empire Springs.

"Why don't you," Carey said in a slightly dismissive tone, "have a seat." She pointed to her right to the living room. "The doctor shall be with you shortly." She then turned and went into the kitchen adjoined to the dining room.

The interior of this house had this woman's fingerprints all over it. The exterior was all Rack: the yard with rock gardens of a variety of green plants and wildflowers, a swath of ivy on trellises at one end of the timber-framed house, a massive chimney made of field stones, a stone path leading to the front porch with a swing chair and a pair of cushioned rocking chairs. And then there were Rack's marijuana plants in the vineyard. Carey didn't seem the type to smoke, but maybe an unguarded side to her was into smoking a joint with her husband when no one was around.

They seemed an odd couple, Carey and Rack, but Maggie put that aside for now, as Rack entered the room.

Rack set up John's car seat in the back of his sedan, and off they went. Rack told Maggie it was no more than a three-hour drive to the medical center, which was on the other side of the freeway from Manhassa Beach. In a little over two years, she had lived through and survived huge life experiences since she had lived there. It seemed a couple of lifetimes ago.

After Carey's snooty act back at the house, it was easy to understand Rack's advances toward her. Maggie wondered if Rack was doing the deed with someone else. And Maggie was beginning to understand why Rack looked forward to sharing a joint and conversation with her—whatever would those two talk about other than their children?

Maggie glanced over her shoulder at John, sound asleep in the back, and then to Rack, who said, "You're being quiet." He slid a look over at Maggie.

"Big day for me and John."

Rack said that they would be putting John through a series of tests, "echo and electrocardiograms, for starters." He went on to explain that Maggie might find it all a bit overwhelming, "but we have the entire ride back for me to go over everything, whatever the results may be."

Maggie and Rack met with Rack's colleague from college, Dr. William Broadhurst. "Call me Bill," he said to Maggie after introductions. He was tall and lean with a finely constructed face and well-formed high brow. But it was his eyes that caught Maggie's attention, intelligent grayish-blue eyes that hinted at a hell-raiser in his youth. He looked like someone with whom Rack would be friends.

Bill went over the schedule. "First a thorough examination, then a series of tests." They were sitting in the doctor's office, Bill behind his desk, Maggie with John in her lap, and Rack seated facing him. Bill glanced down at a medical chart in front of him and then at Maggie. "I've gone over your son's medical history and spoken to Rack." He then placed his elbows on the desk, hands folded under chin. "Anything I say further would strictly be conjecture." He offered his hands, palms up. "By the end of the day, we should know more, much more."

John was squirming in Maggie's arms as though he knew something uncomfortable was about to happen. "Mommy," he said as though giving an order, "we go."

"It won't be until four at the earliest," Bill said, "that we will get the results." He then hit a button on his intercom and asked for a nurse to come into the office.

The door opened as if on cue, and a young woman in a white nurse's uniform entered.

John began squirming even more. "It's okay, John," Maggie said in as calm a voice as she could muster.

"This is Becky," Bill said to Maggie. "She will escort you and John to the lab, where you will have to hand him off at that point."

"No!" John screamed as Maggie stood. "No, Mommy, no!" He seemed to understand or intuit what was happening.

"It's going to be okay, honey," Maggie said. But it wasn't okay; Maggie hadn't told John anything more than that they were taking a trip with Dr. Rack. She had been shoving this moment into the back of her mind since the day her son was born eighteen months ago.

By the time Maggie handed John to Becky outside the lab door, John was in full bloody-murder screaming mode. Maggie thought her heart would break. Rack had told her beforehand about this part of the day, but it was still agonizing.

As the lab door closed and Maggie and Rack began walking down the hall, John's screams grew lighter and lighter until they faded away.

Rack suggested they get something to eat at the cafeteria. Maggie wasn't hungry, as her stomach was a giant pit of turbulence. They were in line with trays sliding them down the metal rails as they passed an array of hot and cold food. It reminded Maggie of high school, with the uniformed women servers wearing hairnets doling out portions of food. And much like high school, Maggie felt there were things going on in her life out of her control.

They took a table in a corner with a view of the freeway in the distance. They were only about ten miles from Manhassa Beach, but it might as well have been a million.

As Maggie picked at her salad, Rack was making short work of a ham and cheese on rye. Maggie pushed her plate away and leaned back in her chair; eating was useless.

"Try and stay calm, Maggie," Rack said as took a hearty bite of his sandwich, swelling his cheek for a moment before three quick chomps and a swallow. He threw his hand in the air. "Easy for me to say, but …" He raised a brow at Maggie as if to say, "Are you with me?"

"It's just that John's grandfather died from this condition in his early forties, and his father has inherited it." Maggie lifted her fork and absentmindedly inspected it. "I've been avoiding facing this since John was born. And now that it is here …"

After lunch and a long, mostly silent, walk around the hospital grounds, they went to the waiting room down the hall from Bill's office. A young couple, no more than twenty, was sitting together holding hands. Rack and Maggie nodded a hello and took a seat across from them. There was a grimness about their faces: the lips set tight, the eyes fraught with fear, and the woman's shoulders hunched up as if preparing to take a body blow.

As Maggie was considering whether she should initiate a conversation, a nurse came into the room and asked the young couple to come with her. The woman sat frozen in her chair as though she could read a vibration of doom emitting from the nurse, an older, heavyset woman with a seen-it-all look about her. But there was something in her voice that had given it away, a tone of such grave seriousness.

"Is my son okay?" the woman said in a raspy whisper. She exchanged a look with the nurse and then turned to her husband. "He's just a baby boy." She looked frantically around the room and caught Maggie's eye. In that moment, Maggie saw and felt the young woman's desperateness.

"The doctor's waiting," the nurse said as she cupped her hand and brought it toward herself for them to come.

The man stood and offered his hand to his wife, who flashed another look at Maggie before standing and walking with her husband out of the room, the door clicking shut behind them.

"That must be the surgery Bill had told me about," Rack said.

Maggie took her eyes off the door and turned to Rack. "Not sure I even want to know what it's about," she said.

Rack lifted a brow as if to say, "Do you want me to continue?"

Maggie nodded, and Rack proceeded to tell her about an infant who was born with multiple heart problems. "Bad valve, weak aortic muscle," he said. "It's a miracle the child survived the birth, Bill told me."

"Did Bill perform the surgery?"

"Yesterday," Rack said. "The baby has been fighting for his life ever since."

The wait was excruciating for Maggie, who couldn't get that young mother out of her mind. By the time they were brought into Bill's office, it was nearly five. John was asleep in the arms of nurse Becky, who handed him over to Maggie.

Maggie could only imagine what her baby boy had gone through as she cradled him in her arms. John woke for a moment, recognized his mother, let out a sigh of relief, and fell back asleep.

Bill was standing behind his desk with hands on the back of his high-back leather chair. He told the nurse she could leave and motioned for Maggie and Rack to sit. A weariness had set in on the heart surgeon;

no longer was there a trace of the former hell-raiser, but in its place a doctor having a long and trying day.

Bill sat and said, "I'll get right to it. There is no evidence that your son has his father's condition." He tapped his index finger on a folder of medical charts on his desk. Inserted in the tab, in bold black letter, was typed the name John O'Brien. "No sign of sick muscle cells." Bill glanced at Rack. "No t-wave inversion," he said before turning his attention to Maggie. "Everything tells me that your son's heart is free and clear of heart disease."

"So," Maggie said as John stirred in her arms, "my son did not inherit his father's heart disease?"

"Yes, that is exactly what I am telling you."

On the ride back, Maggie felt an obvious sense of relief, but at the same time she would never forget this day, the tension of it still stirring in the pit of her stomach.

From the moment she walked into the hospital, with its antiseptic smells, and the medical people bustling by in starched whites, and the sounds of the PA paging a doctor, she realized that today was a day of reckoning. The initial meeting with Bill had brought front and center the reality that John could inherit this life-shortening disease. In the past, Maggie had pushed it back as something to face down the road.

And then there was the young couple in the waiting room, whom it appeared did not have a happy ending in regard to their child—their lives possibly shattered. Maggie thought about asking Bill but decided against it. The nurse and the couple's reaction and the beaten-down weariness in Bill's eyes told her all she needed to know.

She was beginning to understand Johnny's aversion to not only passing his disease on to his progeny, but not wanting to marry. Johnny had lived with this *thing* hanging over his head since the age of ten, and it had not only hung over him like a future guillotine, but had most likely affected the way he saw things in this life. And it would have affected her son for the rest of his life too. But she and John had dodged a bullet, a very big bullet.

They were exiting the freeway, heading east and away from LA, which had a calming effect on Maggie.

"Good day for you and John," Rack said as he came to a traffic light at the top of the exit ramp.

"Yes, indeed," Maggie said with a nod as Rack turned left onto a highway. Off to their right, the Santa Monica Mountains loomed over them like giant sentries. "Thank you for everything. I owe you, Rack. Big-time."

Rack feigned a wolfish smile. "How big?"

"Let me digest the events of today," Maggie said as she checked the backseat, where John was sucking away on a pacifier, looking out the window, an observant squint of wonder in those great blue eyes. She looked back at Rack—*okay?*

His expression was that of doctorly understanding, but mingled with it a shadow of another type of understanding.

They drove in silence for a while, John falling asleep in the backseat, as dusk fell over the land. They were now way outside the pull of Los Angeles, on the two-lane road that had brought them. All the bustle and congestion of the big city were in the rearview mirror, and with it Maggie had settled down. She broke the silence. "May I ask a personal question?"

"Let me guess," Rack said through an emerging smile. "How did I ever end up with Carey?"

Maggie glanced back at John, still asleep, and turned her attention to Rack. "Yes, if I'm not being too nosy."

"Blind date my first year of residency, and we both smoked and drank an abundance of Maui Wowee and cheap-ass wine. Woke up in bed with her the next morning, not remembering a thing."

"Now, let me guess," Maggie said through a revelatory smile. "You weren't planning on seeing her again, but she got pregnant."

Rack shook his head and smiled. He pointed a finger at Maggie and said, "Here's the kicker. We got married, and she had a miscarriage."

"Fate can be ruthless," Maggie said.

"Amen to that."

That Friday, Maggie and Rack shared a joint on his patio. After her first inhale, Maggie said, "You know that no-tell motel on the outskirts of town?"

"Yes," Rack said as he took the doobie from Maggie and held it, waiting.

"One time," Maggie said, "and one time only."

"Okay," Rack said in a careful tone. He took a short drag on the joint, held it for a moment, and exhaled. "Carey is taking the kids to visit her mother over the weekend."

"Sounds like a plan."

That Sunday afternoon, Maggie had asked Millie to watch John while she ran a few errands. Maggie didn't like being dishonest with Millie, but it was just this one time, she told herself.

The Windmill Motel was in the middle of nowhere, off a highway not far from the interstate. Maggie arrived early and parked in the lot, facing the rental office, a separate A-frame with a windmill attached to the roof. The motel itself was a shabby string of rooms in a long building. The place looked nearly deserted, with only a few cars parked at the far end.

Maggie was nervously excited. She hadn't had sex since Chick, their first night together. It had been a good long while. Rack's car pulled into the lot and parked in front of the office. He got out, stood outside his car, and scanned the area. He glanced over at Maggie, but made no acknowledgment. There was something about the way he did this that indicated this wasn't the first time.

When Rack came out of the office, he got in his car and drove to the end of the row of units, Maggie following.

The room was standard issue, with a squishy queen-size bed, which for a moment reminded Maggie of the sofa at Nora's apartment. How long ago and far away that all seemed.

They did it twice, missionary first and then Maggie on top.

After, as they dressed, Rack said, "We could meet here again?" He was buttoning his shirt, his eyes searching Maggie's face.

Maggie had thoroughly enjoyed this wham-bammer with the studly town doc, but, "It's too damn risky, Rack." She was sitting on the edge of the bed, tying the laces to her low-cut sneakers. "But we can still share a doobie." She looked at him—*What do you think?*

"I look forward to your good company."

On the way home, before shifting her mind back to her life as a single mom and employee of Millie's restaurant, Maggie wanted to let her mind linger over her tryst with Rack. Not only was he a stud, but he was hung like a horse and with a wad of girth to boot. The sex had been grinding, grunting sexual pleasure. Maggie's guilt of having a fling with a married man was offset by the fact that he was married to a snob like Carey.

In all their time together, Rack had never complained about his marriage, but he didn't have to. It was evident in the times she had waited on them and their children at the restaurant. Rack conversed with his children, obviously enjoying their company, but when he turned his attention to Carey, the joy left his expression, and in its place was a matter-of-fact look that said, "This is the way it is, and I will make the best of it."

CHAPTER 24

Maggie decided to sell the van. It was a constant reminder of Chick's murder and her near death in Mexico. She could not believe that she had held on to it for going on three years.

It was a Sunday morning, and Maggie was on her way to pick up Raymond, who had volunteered to go with Maggie to the junkyard of a friend, who might be interested in buying it.

Past a bend, the O'Connor house came into view on her right. Every time Maggie drove by, she was duly impressed. There was a tennis court, Olympic-size pool, outdoor stone patio with barbecue pit and redwood furniture, and a landing strip for Mr. O'Connor's Cessna. The house was timber-framed with top-of-the-line material and design: post and beam accentuated by a stone foundation. Millie had attended Christmas parties at the house and told Maggie, "It is right out of *Better Homes and Gardens.*"

But Millie had also told Maggie, "Though extremely generous, the O'Connors are not people you want to cross, especially Brent. Katie suffered a miscarriage the second year they were married." She went on to say that not only did she lose the baby, but could not have children. They were in the vegetable garden picking a bumper crop of bright yellow summer squash.

"Katie was devastated, and Brent got angry. He hired an attorney who specialized in that sort of thing." Millie wiped a splotch of dirt off a squash with a rag and placed it in a wicker basket between two rows.

"The attorney found negligence on the physician's part," Millie said as she and Maggie lifted the basket up the row. "When it was all said and done, the physician lost his license and a ton of money to Brent O'Connor."

Maggie asked if they had considered adoption.

"Don't know, never talked about. But my guess is no," Millie said as she bent down, twisted, and pulled another squash off its stem and put it into the basket. "Brent doesn't seem the type, and what Brent O'Connor wants, he gets."

Past the O'Connors' entrance, Maggie turned off onto a dirt road that wound around to a clearing, park land of tall conifer trees on her left. Up ahead, a small pond came into view, and around it and to the back, situated in a meadow of wild grass, was a cylinder-shaped canvas tentlike structure on a raised platform and with a Plexiglas bubble skylight on top like a crown.

With the mountains looming in the background, it reminded Maggie of a postcard. Raymond came out of the wood-framed door, with a nautical porthole in the center, and stepped down two wooden steps.

"This is wonderful, Raymond," Maggie said, walking up for a closer look. "May I look inside?"

Raymond smiled big, revealing a missing bicuspid. "Abso ... fucking ... lutley." He opened the door and motioned her inside.

"I love it," Maggie said as she took it all in. Hand-woven Indian carpets with zigzag borders and geometric patterns were here and there about the floor, a raised bed-sofa on one side with drawers and built-in cabinets below and attached at the end. There was a bookshelf across the space with an eclectic assortment of books from thick tomes on philosophy to woodworking. Next to the bookshelf was a saggy, cardboard box stuffed with copies of *National Geographic,* and a wood-burning stove in the back corner. The space was in a somewhat disorderly state with clothes lying about and empty beer cans on a low-slung table next to a hardwood-framed easy chair that reminded Maggie of a giant cushion.

"There's a bit of the yin and yang going on in here," Maggie said as she looked upward as light poured through the skylight. "Whatever made you decide to live …" She paused and said, "I mean where did you come up with living in a yurt?"

"I went to Mongolia back in the sixties and lived in one of these with a nomadic tribe for three months."

"Really?" Maggie said, not quite believing.

Raymond went on to explain how he learned to build a yurt, "or *ger*, as the Mongolians say. Yurt is of Turkish origin," he said with a negative squint. "I built this and most of the furniture." He added that Brent O'Connor had offered him free rent. "He told me he liked the idea," Raymond said through an emerging smile, "of having a piece of Mongolian artwork on his land."

They exchanged looks. Maggie was seeing a new side to Raymond.

"Spent three months tramping across the steppe and thought I had found a new life for myself." Raymond's face pinched a little. "Then the cold weather hit." He laughed a self-depreciating laugh. "'To thine own self be true.'" He shook his head at the memory. "I was too damn soft to live in those conditions." He threw his hands out in front of him and said, "Or not crazy enough," he added with a shrug.

They drove north, down into a valley and into a stretch of rolling green hills of farmland and through a small town and then past more farmland until they came to Black Bart's Salvage. Clunker paradise. The place was surrounded by an eight-foot chain-link security fence. Inside were rows and rows of rusty heaps, some fully intact, others picked clean, only the shells remaining. It reminded Maggie of an auto graveyard.

Past the front gate, Raymond told Maggie to park off to the side of a red caboose on cinder blocks; behind it was a barnlike structure made out of corrugated steel. Out of the back door of the caboose emerged a tall, barrel-chested man dressed in dungarees and flannel. He wore his mane of black hair in a ponytail that was matched by a thick, bushy beard, a pirate's beard. All he needed was an eye patch.

"Long time, Raymond," the man said in a gravelly baritone. He flashed a grin at Raymond then turned his attention to Maggie. He cocked his head to the side, the eyes glinting—a big old boy having fun. "Black Bart at your service, ma'am." He rocked back on his heels and offered a jaunty salute off the side of his brow.

Maggie wondered if he was half-drunk or if this was Black Bart being Black Bart. Either way, she liked this large-bodied throwback with a long face and dark thunderclap eyes that were slightly protruding and hinting at intelligence, and the crook of a nose that looked as though it had been chiseled out of stone, and the same for the massive jaw.

Black Bart smiled again at Maggie, and this time gleaming mischief as though he had been testing her. A smile that said you're all right, kiddo. "So I hear you have ..." Black Bart said as his gaze was drifting over toward the van. "Damn, Raymond, you didn't say it was a VW van—a type 2 bus, no less." Black Bart made a fist with his big meaty hand as he shook it overhead, all the while making a beeline toward the van.

Black Bart walked around the vehicle, opening the sliding door and leaning his head inside. He then opened the hood and asked Raymond to start it up. As the engine ran, Black Bart cocked his head off to the side, grinning in appreciation. He closed the hood and ran his thumb under his neck for Raymond to cut the engine.

Black Bart turned his attention to Maggie, who was standing next to Raymond at the driver's door. "Forgive my rudeness, but I have not asked your name." He crossed an arm over his waist and bowed. "But I've had a love affair with these hunks of steel since chickens were crowing on Sourwood Mountain." Black Bart opened his hands to Maggie. "You are?"

"Maggie. Maggie Meyers."

"Maggie Meyers, huh," Black Bart said, slanting a look at Raymond and then back at Maggie. "That's a great name," he said in a ringing tone. There seemed to be many facets to this bear of a man called Black Bart.

"Interested in buying the van, Bart?" Raymond asked.

Black Bart puckered his lips, nodding as though an idea had suddenly come to him. "How about a trade?"

"Hah," Raymond cracked. "Come on, Bart, this is where cars come to die."

Black Bart squiggled his index finger at Maggie. "Follow me, my dear." He threw a look at Raymond, and said out of the side of his mouth, "And you too, my friend. Allow me to show you where cars also come to be reborn."

Inside the barn were cars of all types, three deep and ten to a row.

"You've upgraded, Bart," Raymond said as he walked down a row checking a long and sleek gray sedan.

"That's a '34 Studebaker Dictator and not for sale," Black Bart said as Raymond stuck his head in the driver's window.

The space was a combination storage room and garage, as there were car lifts on the far end, and along the back wall a long workbench littered with batteries, gaskets, hoses, and such.

"Maggie," Black Bart said, "take your time and see if there is something you like." He raised his hand. "Within reason, that is."

Maggie and Raymond walked down all the rows, and when they finished, Maggie said, "I like the woody." She thought it was a Chevrolet but wasn't sure. But she loved the wood paneling that went so perfectly with the contoured, baby-blue body, and then the whitewall tires and lift gate in the back. She loved this car. She had to have this car.

"Oh, that's a very fine car."

"What year is it, Bart?" Raymond said as he lifted the hood.

"Fifty-one Mercury."

Raymond glanced at Maggie, and she gave him a nod as if to say *permission granted*. "Well, Bart, tell us what you have in mind."

After much finagling back and forth between Black Bart and Raymond, Maggie agreed to pay $500 cash for the deal. But first she wanted a test drive. "No problem," Black Bart said as he handed her the keys. The car rode great, and Black Bart even told Maggie that if she had any problems in the first year to bring it by, and he'd fix it no charge, "If in reason, of course," he added. Maggie wasn't sure what was *in reason*, but she trusted Black Bart.

So off Maggie and Raymond drove with a nagging part of her past now in her past.

CHAPTER 25

Millie had given Maggie opportunities to experiment on some dinner specials and soups, and all went over well with the customers, but one was a big hit. She had made a chicken tortilla soup that included a cilantro/lime juice/avocado-based marinade, and to top it off she steamed the marinated chicken in a metal colander to make her own broth. This was a recipe of Maya's that Maggie tweaked a bit. It was so good that Millie suggested Maggie enter it in the cooking contest at the Autumn Apple Festival up north in Gliberville, California. "I hear it's a lot of fun, and with some real good cooks," Millie told her.

Maggie liked the idea of entering a cooking contest. Not only would it give her a chance to break the routine of work and child-rearing, but a chance to meet other people interested in her passion—cooking. Millie had told her that there were other festivals within a hundred-mile radius of Empire Springs and that if Maggie wanted to take a few days off from time to time, she would be more than glad to look after John, whom she doted on like a grandmother.

At two and half years old, John was the spitting image of his handsome father: acres of wavy black hair, pinch of pink in the cheeks, and eyes that bespoke kindness of heart and an unconquerable spirit. He was the embodiment of Johnny O'Brien, her son, John O'Brien.

Maggie was still torn about Johnny not knowing he had a son. But when she escaped from Mexico alive, it was as though she had begun a new life, a second chance. Returning back to her past remained a path she did not want to go down. She knew it was not logical, but there was some force within her that said no turning back. Johnny O'Brien and Bethesda, Maryland, were in her past. Fate had spoken.

Millie had told Maggie that she had a good life in Empire Springs and shouldn't go stirring up a hornet's nest from her past. They were playing gin at Millie's house on a Sunday evening at the kitchen table. "He made a decision that he didn't want you in his life," Millie said as she removed a card from her hand, thought better of it, and put another card down. "Even though his intentions were good and for your sake, he was telling you to move on with your life."

Rack had told Maggie that Johnny's heart condition could possibly weigh heavily on his mind, not only the fact that he could die within the next ten years, "but, medically speaking, situations like this often create a fatalistic persona." They were sharing a joint on Rack's patio. Maggie took a toke and passed it to Rack. "Are you saying it might not be good for John to be around that environment?"

"Possible," Rack said as if considering. He took a long pull on the joint. He flicked an ash and looked out at his vineyard, rows of vines clinging to the wooden posts. "Very possible," Rack said with a nod of the head. "I did further research on John's father's condition. It's not only rare but a ticking time bomb after forty."

But at some point she would have to tell John about his father. And also, very possibly, Maggie realized he would want to meet his father. That is how Johnny would have been. But that was down the road, and for now … Maggie would put it on the back burner.

CHAPTER 26

The back of the woody was packed with a folding table, an assortment of cooking utensils, a four-quart cooking pot that Millie lent Maggie, a cooler containing quart jars of her chicken tortilla soup stock that she had cooked back at the restaurant, diced chicken wrapped in tin foil that she had made the stock from, and the other vegetable and herbal ingredients stored in either baggies or tin foil, plus two cans of black beans, avocados, and limes. She had also purchased a Coleman gas stove with dual burners, which Wilbur showed her how to start and operate on the back porch of Millie's Place. She liked the idea of owning her own little stove. It made her feel that she was serious about cooking competitions.

Gliberville was a hundred miles north of Empire Springs, and Maggie had reserved a room at a bed-and-breakfast for both Friday and Saturday after Millie had convinced her to take the time off and get away on her own for a few days. "The restaurant and John will be just fine without you."

After Millie double-checked that Maggie hadn't forgotten anything, Maggie kissed John goodbye, not sure what to expect: Would he cry that his mother was leaving him for the first time? Would he give her the silent treatment as though she were deserting him? But much to Maggie's surprise, he wasn't a bit frightened that Mommy was leaving him for the first time. "Fun, Mommy, fun."

Part of Maggie was relieved that John took her departure so well, but another part was conflicted that he wasn't in the least concerned.

Millie held John in the crook of her arm, his little head resting on her shoulder, her white hair in direct contrast to Maggie's black-haired son. John was perfectly comfortable in the arms of his "Mill Mill."

Millie seemed to read Maggie's concern. "Think fun, Maggie, think fun."

"Okay, fun it is." Maggie smiled at Millie and then her son. And with that she was off, Millie waving John's hand until they disappeared from the rearview mirror.

It was a two-and-a-half-hour drive to Gliberville, and it came over Maggie that this was her first time on the road alone since she departed Mexico three years ago. Selling the van had, as she had hoped, eliminated the constant reminder of the murders and those murderous banditos. *That was in a past life,* she told herself, as she turned onto a two-lane highway.

Though, from time to time, Maggie did wonder how Maya was doing. If she really went to stay with her cousin in Argentina—she thought so. Staying at what was left of El Rancho did not seem an option. Even if she rebuilt, the memories would have swallowed her up, as resilient as that good woman was. If anyone deserved a bit of happiness in their life, it was Maya.

Happiness seemed something that Maggie was basking in at this stage of her life. John was now a little person who was developing a vocabulary. Rack told Maggie that he was advanced in not only his physical skills—he could throw and catch a tennis ball—but he could construct complete sentences when the mood struck him. Oftentimes John kept it simple if that was all that was needed. "Fun, Mommy, fun."

It had rained last night, and the sun was out in all its glory, its golden light glittering in the roadside puddles and the silver roofs of the farmhouses and barns that flickered in view between the red and golden-yellow foliage. It was as though Maggie were driving through a fairyland. She remember the Robert Frost poem about the fork in the road, and she had a gut feeling that her life was about to take another sharp turn.

CHAPTER 27

G liberville was located in a valley with a vista of low-slung hills in the distance. The town proper was bigger than Empire Springs; of course, just about any place was, but still maintained a similar small-town charm but in a more upscale fashion.

Maggie drove down Main Street past a row of retail shops and businesses. There were benches every so often between the sidewalk and street, and flags with Autumn Apple Festival flapped gently in a breeze from wrought iron lampposts. A restaurant's outdoor dining area had red umbrellas with Autumn Apple Festival scrolled in white. At the end of the row was the town hall anchored by a stone base, stucco second story adorned with turrets and arches, and capped by a cupola and clock.

The Crawford House B&B was a two-story clapboard structure. A brick walk led to a grand front porch with curved-back swings on both ends. Stone-bordered beds of hydrangeas, hostas, and colorful flowers were discreetly situated in a grassless front yard. A stone pathway led to a latticed arbor of ivy, which led to the rear of the house.

As Maggie reached to open the front door, it opened. A man stood at the threshold, a startled expression on his face. "Oh, sorry," he said. "Didn't know you were there."

His voice had that nasally tone of East Coast elite. He was young, younger than Maggie, with a high forehead and light brown hair, a broad likable face, and thick roly-poly body. He whisked away a lank of hair dangling over his brow, standing there as though deciding what his next move should be. "Let me guess," he said through an emerging smile. "I bet we're in the same boat—cooking competition."

"Yes," Maggie said, returning the smile.

He had a look that she had come to know over the years: *I'd like to get to know you look.* He extended his hand, "I'm Peter Vanderson."

Maggie felt the touch of calloused fingertips on the back of her hand, a sure sign of someone spending time in a kitchen handling cutting knives and hot dishes. "Maggie Meyers here." Maggie smiled again, a reassuring smile. "I'm entering my chicken tortilla soup," she said with raised brow as if to say, "Your turn."

"Texas chili," Peter said. "First contest?"

"Yes, how did you know?"

Peter shrugged and said, "I don't know … just a guess." He shrugged again and made a face as though to say here goes. "Would you be my guest for dinner tonight?"

Maggie's room was small with furniture that bordered on antique. There was a refurbished armoire with flatiron latches, a desk with many compartments and drawers that reminded her of her grandparents' furnishings, and a canopied queen bed. As for a bathroom, there was one at each end of the hall. *No biggie,* Maggie thought as she looked out her window that had a view of the backyard with a brick terrace, pond, and pedestal birdbath, all under the foliage of a massive elm tree. Toward the back of the yard sat a tin-roofed gazebo. The view made her feel special that she, Maggie Meyers, was about to enter her first cooking competition, but definitely not her last. She could hear the judge announcing, "The winner is Maggie Meyers's chicken tortilla soup."

But Maggie wondered if semi pre-made entries were frowned upon by the judges. There were many things Maggie was curious about, but she would be able to find this all out tonight at dinner with Peter.

The Californian Restaurant was an upscale establishment with a teardrop-shaped oak bar in the front room; overhead the bar was a disc-shaped dome overhang with a series of drawings of cowboys breaking horses in corrals. What really drew Maggie's eye was the golden-ocher color of the artwork—beautiful it was.

Peter and Maggie decided to sit at the bar and have a drink before dinner. Everything about this place reeked of the good life from the unisex wait staff in white shirts and bow ties, to the oak wine rack behind the bar with hand-carved grape motifs on the twin-paned glass doors, to the people themselves dressed in casual chic—women in cashmere sweaters and designer jeans, the men in penny loafers and polo shirts. The clientele reminded Maggie of the moneyed horse crowd back home in Potomac, Maryland.

"Do you like wine?" Peter asked Maggie, as he pulled back her dark-stained ladder-back chair, with plush leather cushions, at the end of the nearly packed bar.

"Cabernet," Maggie said. "You pick."

"All righty then," Peter said as he sat and raised a casual finger to the bartender. He did not seem out of place in this environment, and Maggie got the sense that he came from money. Something about the confident air he exuded as he questioned the bartender on the wines. And the insouciant manner in which he dressed, not shabby but sort of upscale downscale: sneakers without socks, corduroy trousers, and a tweed sport coat with untucked dress shirt.

After Peter tested the wine and nodded his approval, he raised his glass to Maggie. "Cheers."

Maggie took a sip; it was wonderful wine, full-bodied and earthy with a hint of black cherry.

Peter told Maggie that he was a line cook at a French restaurant in San Bernardino. "Really?" Maggie said. "What's it like?"

"Hard work, and the chef is a prickly Frenchman," Peter said. "But I'm learning things I never learned in school."

It turned out that Peter, who was from upstate New York, had graduated from Cornell two years ago with a degree in culinary arts.

"Oh," Maggie said, trying to suppress how impressed she was by this. And it dawned on her that she was six years older than Peter. Not that she was bothered by it.

She was still deciding whether she was going to sleep with him, and for some reason that was a point in his favor, but definitely not tonight; tomorrow was a big day.

Over dinner, Peter explained to Maggie what to expect at the cooking competition as far as setting up and presentation: "Judges like pretty," he said. He ran through a few other dos and don'ts such as, "We'll need to arrive early and pick the right spot to set up our equipment." Peter went on to explain that he tried to get his dish somewhere in the middle of the tasting, so that when the judges tried it, "their palates weren't saturated with other foods, but they had sampled enough to find mine worth remembering."

Peter also mentioned that rumor had it that after this year, all chili and soup entries would be made from scratch. "Only chili contest I've ever entered that allows partial food preparation ahead of time."

Maggie asked if the judges held it against soup broths prepared beforehand.

"If it has that left-over aftertaste," Peter said. "But I've seen contestants devastated after not getting it all done in time and being disqualified." He stared into his wine for a moment and turned his attention back to Maggie. "First contest, not a bad idea to prepare the broth ahead of time, assuring you will get this one under your belt."

The dinner was excellent: Maggie had lobster bisque—Peter insisted she order it—herb salad with honey mustard vinaigrette, and grilled salmon. Peter ordered a rack of lamb with rosemary roasted potatoes and shallot vinaigrette.

During the meal, Maggie told Peter little about herself other than where she grew up and where she currently lived and worked. She didn't mention John.

Peter seemed to sense that she was holding back but wisely did not push the subject, another point for the young line cook.

He was an easy conversationalist and had some humorous stories about working for a French chef: "When Jean Louis gets angry he curses in French, spittle drooling on his chin, cheeks fire-engine red as though ready to blow his starched white torque."

Maggie thoroughly enjoyed listening to Peter talk about his kitchen experiences, and at the same time she made mental notes about how the kitchen was run and food prepared. Peter went on to say that he wasn't really a big fan of French food, "but I wanted to learn from the best, and the French are *the* best."

After dinner, Peter suggested they meet for breakfast at the B&B at seven, "And go from there." His expression had changed as tomorrow seemed front and present on his mind. This young guy took his cooking seriously, and that was another big point in Maggie's book.

The Autumn Apple Festival was held on the outskirts of town at the Gliberville Municipal Park, a lovely expanse of ball fields and picnic areas. A raised wooden platform had been set up in front of a large canopy tent, where the judges would taste the entries. Bales of hay that Peter said were for seating were being unloaded in front of the platform.

There were rows of booths, with red-and-white-striped awnings for ring toss, shooting gallery, and milk bottle toss; food vendors selling caramel candy, apple cider, hot dogs and hamburgers; and arts and crafts with artists, wood craftsmen, and weavers arranging their displays.

Off to the side of the tent, a DJ was running an electrical cord to a massive generator. This was much more than a cooking contest, and part of Maggie was worried that the contest would just be a minor side event.

There were two cooking contests: desserts that were prepared ahead of time, and soup or chili. In Maggie's competition, each contestant had to prepare seven separate bowls of his or her dish—five for the judges, one for the emcee, and one to be presented by the emcee for the winning entry.

Peter asked Maggie if she had a copy of her recipe.

"Oh no," Maggie said in a panicky voice. "I left it in my room."

"Don't worry," Peter said as he removed a pen and spiral notebook from a briefcase. "I was a Boy Scout, always prepared."

Maggie wrote down *Ingredients* and listed every one, checking twice. She then wrote down the directions of making her chicken tortilla soup.

While Maggie checked over her recipe, Peter hoisted his gas grill up on his table and then unloaded the contents of a cooler: jars of diced tomatoes—"homegrown and cut myself"—plump cloves of garlic, a mound of thickly spooled ground chuck, a plastic container of lard, a metal shaker of spices, dried jalapeno peppers, red chilies, a jar of dried herbs … "And last but not least," he said as he held up a bar of dark chocolate as if presenting exhibit A, "my secret weapon."

Peter then opened a metal case containing an impressive array of cutlery, from which he removed a paring and chopping knife and placed them on a cutting board.

After an official picked up the recipes from each contestant, they were told that they had three hours to prepare their dishes. Some of the contestants had brought huge gas grills, refrigerators, and a couple even had sinks. *These folks are serious,* Maggie thought as she peeked around at her competitors.

Maggie stoked the pump plunger on the Coleman just as Wilbur had showed her. She lit the stove with a long match—Wilbur had given her a box of matches—then added the chicken stock, diced chicken, and seasoning into the pot. On a cutting board, she then began dicing onions, garlic, jalapenos, tomatoes, cilantro … This was work, but this was fun work, competing with other folks who also had a passion for cooking.

While she was dicing and adding ingredients to her pot, Maggie peeked from time to time at Peter chopping and dicing away: Vidalia onions, green and red pepper, and garlic with lightning-quick precision. He was wearing the same sneakers from last night, white socks, jeans, and an apron over a flannel shirt, sleeves rolled to the elbows.

Peter continued his rapid pace, with a bon mot every now and then: "It's a hanging offense in Texas to add beans to chili."

By the third hour, Peter's chili was taking on a deep, rich, brownish-amber color that looked delicious.

With five minutes to go before the three-hour limit, Peter grated a bar of Wisconsin cheddar—"Best cheese in America"—and sprinkled it on top of his seven paper bowls of chili and then added a dollop of sour cream.

Meanwhile, Maggie had ladled her soup and topped each one off with avocado slices and grated Monterrey jack cheese, and grilled tortilla strips handmade at Millie's Place that she had cooked in vegetable oil on a frying pan on her Coleman.

After their entries were taken to the tent and the awaiting judges, Maggie took in the festival that was now in full swing: the DJ was blasting away oldies; people were everywhere, an uproar here and there of laughter at one of the amusement booths rising above the din of shouting children and happy talk. The sun was out in a clear blue sky, and the air was dry and cool, and the good folks of Gliberville seemed to draw a vigor and vitality from it.

While Maggie and Peter waited for the results, people were allowed to come into the cooks' row and buy a bowl with wooden coins that they had purchased. Across from the soup and chili row was the dessert row, and Maggie noted that it was mostly women while hers was mostly men, some in teams, a few with a woman. But soups and chili seemed to be a male's domain.

"What's that?" A white-haired grandma-looking woman asked Maggie, leaning her head nearly into the pot of soup.

"Tortilla chicken soup."

The woman tweaked her nose and squinted as though she had never heard such a thing. "Really?" she said as she slid over to inspect Peter's chili. "Now that's more like it." She handed Peter a coin, and he asked her if she would like cheese or sour cream.

"Lord no," the woman said peering over her wire-rim glasses at Peter. "Good chili don't need any condiments."

Peter ladled a plastic bowl and flashed a grin at Maggie and then the woman. "Here you go, ma'am," he said through a sunny smile, but with a bit of a boyish smirk in the corner of his mouth.

The woman threw a look at Peter as though to ascertain if he was messing with her. She then dipped her spoon into the chili and held it up for inspection, blew on it, and at last stuck the spoon in her mouth. She looked hard at Peter for a moment and then burst out, "Hey now, sonny boy, that's some mighty fine chili."

Maggie and Peter stood at the table as people walked up and down the row looking over their choices before deciding. Peter told Maggie not to get upset about comments or attitudes. "Most folks are real friendly at these events ..." He paused as a young couple came up to Maggie. The woman was in her mid-twenties, small and thin, with autumn-colored hair and a nervousness about her. "Chicken tortilla soup, right?" She reminded Maggie of a worried rabbit.

"Yes," Maggie said. "Would you like a bowl?"

"Two bowls," the husband said and lifted his chin toward the tortillas and other condiments, "and with the works, please." He was a big, broad-shouldered man, and his attitude was easygoing, everything about him the opposite of his wife.

"I've had chicken soup all my life," the man said pointing a spoonful at Maggie, "and this is some of the best ..." He took another bite and finished his thought, "if not the best I've ever eaten."

Maggie smiled big at the man. She felt as though she were floating above the ground. "Thank you," she said as she peeked at Peter, who beamed a congratulatory smile.

And so it went. Maggie got into the spirit of the festival and chatted, not only with potential customers, but the other contestants. There was a happy-go-lucky spirit about this melting pot of cooks. Some had a countrified air about them and twang to their voices that hinted at the old west, and others appeared more upscale, not in their clothes, but more the way they spoke in a clear, disciplined voice: "The key to a successful dish is a proper distribution of ingredients and at the proper time," one cook said. He was the leader of a group of two men and a woman who had driven all the way from San Francisco. They had cooked both a soup and chili entry and had top-of-the-line equipment: four-burner gas grill, glistening cutlery that any chef would be proud to own, and a battery-operated mini-fridge. But there was not a bit of snobbery about them or any of the other cooks.

When the DJ announced the judges had the results, Maggie and Peter took a seat on a bale of hale. The head judge handed the results to the DJ standing on the platform. He gave a short speech about what a successful festival it was and how many "wonderful entries" there were this year.

As the DJ prepared to announce the results of the dessert entries, Maggie picked out of a few of the dessert entrants. Over the course of the day, she had glanced across at these women, some dressed in jeans and work shirts, others in frilly blouses and skirts, but all of them seemed to have a similar trait of down-home competence, as though they led orderly, proper lives with nary a miscue along way. Maggie imagined them marrying their high school sweethearts and starting a family, working and scraping their way in this life, and attending the same church every Sunday. They had chosen the road most traveled—the safest road—and believed in order and routine, and cooked their desserts accordingly. They *were* the polar opposite of Maggie Meyers. *Except for one thing,* Maggie thought, *a joy of cooking.*

After the top three winning desserts were announced, and the winner had received a trophy and winnings—seventy-five dollars for first—it was time for soup or chili.

Finishing in third place was the team from San Francisco for their fish stew. The leader came up and accepted his award with a wry smile as though he had expected to take first place. At this point, Maggie had no such allusion. Though good, her soup stock had not maintained the freshness and vigor that it had when she had prepared it back at Millie's Place; something had been lost along the way. And the big man who had told her how wonderful it was, she now figured, probably said that to every cook.

A vegetable beef soup cooked by a team of local men finished second.

Now the big moment: Maggie glanced at Peter, who had a look of calm anticipation—*if I win, great, if not there is always next time.* She had tried his chili and the old grandma had been right—it was mighty fine. Part of her wished for Peter to win and another competitive side didn't.

"And the winner is"—the DJ looked over the audience like a bad actor trying to build up suspense—"Peter Vanderson's Texas chili."

"How about that," Peter said to Maggie as he stood and walked up and received his trophy and one-hundred-dollar check. While the crowd clapped its approval, Maggie was already thinking about what she'd do differently at next year's competition.

On the drive back to the B&B in Peter's car, Maggie placed her hand on the back of Peter's neck. "Congratulations, champ." Maggie had more or less accepted the fact that she had not won and did not deserve to win, but she was still trying to come to terms with Peter, twenty-four-year-old Peter, winning the whole shebang.

But Maggie had also stored her disappointment into a little compartment in the back of her head, as she had decided to enjoy the unfolding of the evening's events. Peter had suggested a local restaurant, "With an old-time atmosphere and little pretension—a let-your-hair-down kinda place with a great bar."

And Maggie had her own suggestion that she would bring up at the appropriate time: Peter's room was where they would do the deed, leaving her the option of returning to her bed if she so desired.

Back at the B&B, Peter helped Maggie store her gear in the woody. "My father is a car nut, and I've inherited the disease," he said as he closed the back hatch and began walking around the car, as if seeing it for the first time, checking out the rear taillights. "Yeah," he said in an appreciative tone, as he ran his fingertips over a bolt in the rear bumper, "billet 303 stainless steel."

He then had asked if he could start it up. "Built like a tank but purrs like a kitten," Peter said with hands gripping the steering wheel as he listened to the engine. He got out and ran his hand over the two-tone wood paneling. "This car is going to be worth big money some day." He tapped the roof and said, "If you put it in storage and wait twenty years, you would make a very, *very* nice profit."

Maggie loved the look of the car, but it got poor mileage and it took an effort to turn the steering wheel. "Something to consider," she said in a voice that indicated a change of subject. "Let's celebrate the victory of Chef *Pierre*," Maggie said as she took Peter's chin in her hand to draw his attention away from the car. "And determine a proper reward." Maggie's face was in Peter's, her beguiling eyes reeling him in.

A look of discovery came over Peter's face. "That sounds like a proper idea." His voice was a whisper as though he had lost his breath for a moment.

The Millhouse Pub was at the other end of town, and Peter and Maggie walked over, since the proprietor of the B&B had told them that parking, "in our little entertainment side of town," was hard to find on Saturday nights and especially during the festival week.

It was an enjoyable walk from one end of Gliberville to the other. Dusk had settled in, and the shops were aglow in yellow and gold, the mountains in the distance like dark humps against a purple-streaked sky. There was a chill in the air, and Maggie wore cords and a cotton-knit pullover sweater over a long sleeve T-shirt. She had thought about something tighter and more seductive, but she went for comfort instead. Peter was dressed in his sneakers, no socks, and cords, and a Cornell sweatshirt with red lettering. "I'm wearing my school colors to celebrate," he said, "carnelian and white."

He was freshly shaven, and his slightly damp hair was combed, and Maggie thought she got a whiff of Old Spice.

On the way over, they talked about the day's events and people they had met. Peter told Maggie that this was his first win, "Had a few seconds," he said as they stopped in front of a clothing store with mannequins in the window: the males in turtlenecks, the women in cashmere sweaters. "I think it was my secret weapon," Peter said turning to Maggie.

"Dark chocolate," Maggie said as she admired a turquoise hand-knitted sweater.

"No," Peter said. "You're my secret weapon."

Maggie looked at Peter to see if he was kidding, but his expression let her know that he was not. "I'm honored," she said.

"No," Peter said, "I'm the one who is honored."

The Millhouse was a helluva-good-time place. A barrel of peanuts was in the corner, shells littered about the wood-planked floor. The walls were old brick, and massive timbers ran the length of the high ceiling. In the center of the space was a circular bar, and along the walls were round tables made of whiskey barrels topped off with round oak tops edged with a metal band—each with four stools—and a backroom with a smaller bar and picnic tables covered with red gingham tablecloths.

A couple got up from the bar to be seated for dinner, and Maggie and Peter slipped into their seats. "It was a good year for the orchards," Peter said as he raised a finger to get the bartender's attention. "Can you feel the vibe?"

"Yes," Maggie said as she soaked in the hum of energy emitting from this rustic establishment of wood and masonry. "It's almost like a silent buzz, if you know what I mean."

The bartender came over, and Peter said to Maggie, "I feel like a cold beer."

"Make that two chillys," Maggie said.

Peter ordered and turned to Maggie. "Chillys? I've never heard that usage for beer."

"Oh," Maggie said as she leaned back as a frosted mug of beer was placed in front of her. She curled her hand around the icy-cold glass and lifted it to Peter. "It's a Bethesda thing."

Peter clinked her glass. "Bethesda thing, huh," he said, nodding as if he had just figured something out.

Maggie drank some of her beer. She looked around the room, the happy faces, the gurgles of laughter, and it took her back to McDonald's Raw Bar, and the camaraderie of Johnny O'Brien and his circle of friends, a circle she had entered and loved being in.

She had sensed at the time that it was a once-in-a-lifetime opportunity, not only Johnny but his group of friends. Maggie had gotten along fine with the girlfriends and wives, but it was the boys, her boys from Bethesda, that she most enjoyed. Once at a party, Danny McKenzie said something to Maggie that she would never forget. "You're a guy's kinda of woman, Maggie." He looked at her to see if she was catching his drift, and he then said, "Not just your looks, but you're spirit. I love your spirit."

The bartender came over, and Peter ordered two more beers.

"So how did a guy from Upstate New York end up in the unglamorous part of California?"

"Nepotism." Peter hunched his shoulders as if to say, *That's the way it is.* "The owner of the restaurant I work at went to Cornell with my father."

Maggie laughed. "Take it anyway you can get it."

"My plan is to learn the business, not only in the kitchen but how to operate." Peter paused as the bartender served their fresh drinks. He nodded a thank-you and said, "I want to own my own restaurant."

"What type of food?"

"Southwestern cuisine," Peter said as he lifted his mug and took a long swallow. He wiped his bottom lip with the back of his forefinger. "It can be made inexpensively in many instances, and there is a diversity of flavors that interests me."

They exchanged a look, and in it something passed between them. Maggie lifted her brow shrewdly and said, "You mean like my soup?"

The overcast, drizzly sky matched Maggie's mood. It had been a great weekend in Gliberville, and now she was back on the road heading home. She was driving south through farmland, herds of cattle and sheep, and a field of corn stubble that a farmer on a tractor was tilling.

Scenes from last night drifted in her mind: the great time at the Millhouse, Peter and her drinking too many beers, eating burgers and fries for dinner, and a couple of shots at the bar. They talked mostly about cooking. Maggie liked the way Peter's mind worked in that regard. He had a plan to work five years, save money, and then head to Portland, Oregon. "I been there twice," he had said as he swiveled around on his bar stool, his gaze settling on Maggie with casual alertness. "It's a different kind of place, sort of has a blue-collar, bohemian aspect to it that appeals to me."

Peter seemed to have no interest in probing Maggie about herself. Or was he tuned in to her lack of interest in discussing these matters?

Outside the Millhouse, Peter had taken Maggie's hand in his as they walked back to the B&B in silence, but in that silence was an understanding that they were not done with each other.

At the front door, Peter slipped his key in the lock and turned to Maggie. "My room or yours?"

Maggie was entering a one-traffic-light town, more a series of nondescript buildings: She passed Anderson Fuel and Feed, Gibbs Hardware ... At the end of town she stopped at a red light with nary a car on the road. At a one-pump gas station, a teenager in a ball cap pumped gas for a woman behind the wheel, primping herself in the rearview mirror—a string of pearls around the neck, bright red lipstick, and her hair in a neat little bun. She had the reserved and respectful look of someone about to go to church.

The woman looked over at Maggie in her baby-blue woody and raised her brow as she looked over the car and its occupant. It wasn't a condescending look, but more an *I didn't expect to see you here* look.

This seemed a lifeless place, hardly a soul about and with none of the sense of community of Gliberville or that hum of energy. It seemed a going-through-the-motions place.

Oh, but last night there was no going through the motions. Maggie and Peter got it on big-time in his bed. Peter was an eager and passionate lover, if a bit inexperienced—"You're my third girl," he told Maggie in the morning after their third go-round.

He was her first chubby. She remembered a girl back in college who liked to date heavy guys, and a girlfriend designated her a *chubby chaser.*

Maggie's lovers had been for the most part lean and/or muscular; a few weren't, but none had been fat. She hadn't consciously made that decision; it seemed rather she was drawn to a certain type or possibly them to her. But all that was before Mexico and before she had entered her new life. It wasn't as though Peter had folds and folds of fat layering his body, but more an excess of girth. The sex was more than satisfactory, though part of her didn't get off completely as on her one-time stand with Rack and his big asset.

But Peter had an equanimity about him that she found appealing. In the morning after she had dressed, she turned to Peter lying on his side, hand under chin, watching her with a look of composed satisfaction. "I should tell you," Maggie said, "that I have a young son."

"What's his name?" Peter said.

"John O'Brien."

"John ... O'Brien," he said stringing the name out. Peter's sleepy eyes brightened, and he smiled a gorgeous smile that seemed to offer some heightened sensitivity of understanding. "I hope we can meet someday."

"I would like that," Maggie said.

The light turned green, and Maggie accelerated slowly; a dull gray silo up ahead on her left seemed to loom over this little nothing place. She and Peter's schedules and their distance apart would be a challenge, "About a hundred miles," he had told her. But he could arrange to work extra hours to get a weekend or a couple of days in a row off, "if you'd like to see me again."

CHAPTER 28

When Maggie pulled into the driveway, Millie and Daniel were in the front yard raking leaves, John with a baby rake mimicking his Mill Mill and Dan Dan's raking motions. "Mommy, Mommy," John shrieked as he ran up to the car. It was amazing to Maggie the coordinated way in which her toddler son could move. He had none of the typical herky-jerky toddler movement, but rather a fluidity of motion that the boy had inherited from his athletic father.

Maggie lifted John up, and he wrapped his arms around her neck, his rainwater-soft baby smell filling her nostrils. "Good to have my boy back in my arms," Maggie said as she gave him a big squeeze before putting him down.

Millie and Daniel came over and greeted Maggie.

"How did you do, in the cooking competition?" Daniel said. He was now over six feet tall with broad shoulders and was a starting end on the high school football team.

Maggie shook her head and squinted a smile. "No go, Daniel, but I did learn a few things."

"Rake, Dan Dan, rake," John said as he took Daniel's hand, and back to the leaves they went.

"Did you enjoy it, Maggie?" Millie said.

"Yes, it was a lot of fun," Maggie said as she watched John standing alongside Daniel trying to mimic his raking motion. Maggie told Millie about her weekend, including her liaison with Peter.

Millie's eyes grew wide with mock astonishment. "I thought you'd have fun, girl," Millie said through a laugh, "but not that much."

They both burst out in snorting laughter. Maggie asked about how John did, and Millie gave a complete rundown of activities from day care to bedtime story. "He told me the first night he wanted his mommy, but I told him she needed some time off on her own."

"Yeah," Maggie said.

"He made a pouty face at first," Millie said, glancing a look over at John running his hands through the pile of leaves and tossing them in the air, "and then looked at me with those baby blues, and a frown came over his face, and he told me he was glad for his mommy."

Maggie brought her hand over her heart. "Aww," she said as she scanned the yard: azalea bushes along the white picket fence bordering the neighbor's yard beginning to shed their violet leaves, the oak tree with clusters of acorns scattered underneath, and the moderately sized timber-framed house Millie's husband had built. Maggie took a breath and said, "So how were things at the restaurant?"

Millie paused for a moment and slid a look over at the leaf pile where Daniel was raking away, stretching his long arms out gathering the yellow and red leaves into the growing pile. John was now sitting in the middle of the pile scooping up leaves and dropping them over his head.

Millie then said, "All hell blew up Friday night." She went on to say that Carey came in during happy hour and went over to the bar and "called Angie McCrowley out in no uncertain terms."

Maggie felt her jaw drop. "The librarian?"

"Yes indeed, and then Carey threw photos at Angie, of Rack and her naked as jaybirds in a compromising position at the Windmill Motel." Millie looked at Maggie. "You know the motel I'm talking about, over near the interstate?"

It turns out Carey had been suspicious of Angie and hired a private eye to follow her around.

Millie made a face as though she had more to tell. "And then Carey went tearing into Angie with fists flying."

"You're kidding," Maggie said as it came over her that this horrifying moment could have been hers.

"Wilbur hustled out from behind the bar and hoisted Carey off a screaming, snarling Angie, who was kicking and scratching up a storm."

Maggie and Millie both checked on John simultaneously and then turned back to each other. "It was one hell of a catfight," Millie said. She went on to explain that after things calmed down, Wilbur escorted Carey to the door, and Angie sat back at the bar, inspecting her shattered eyeglasses.

"She squinted a bat-blind look at Wilbur and then at a crew of guys from O'Connor Construction slouched around the bar, all them with this look of fascination as if they were seeing Angie in a totally different light. She then said something that made me laugh," Millie said, shaking her head at the memory. "'I never thought my nearsightedness would be a blessing, but it's hard to feel a sense of embarrassment when one cannot see one's detractors.'"

"She then ordered a shot of rye, downed it, and said something about a winged cupid painting her blind."

Maggie tried to speak, but she had no words. She stared at Millie and finally said, "Wow."

"Here's the real kicker," Millie said as she flicked a loose strand of hair from her forehead. "Rack and Carey, who had a bright red scratch mark the length of her forehead, came into the restaurant for Saturday supper with the two children and acted for all the world as if nothing had happened."

Millie went on that a friend of hers, who knew Carey, told Millie that Rack gave his word no more shenanigans.

Maggie realized that her doobie times with Rack were over, and in a way she was relieved. It had run its course. She had dodged another bullet in her life. Big-time.

CHAPTER 29

By the time John entered kindergarten, in September 1983, Maggie and Peter had been in a long-distance relationship for nearly three years. Things had changed not only at Millie's home, with Daniel having departed for college two years ago, but Millie decided to shorten the hours of operation at the restaurant from eleven to nine to noon to eight. "That's twelve hours a week we can have to ourselves," Millie told Maggie. "Life's too short to spend practically every waking hour at the restaurant." Millie was dicing carrots, in preparation for a weekly special, Meyers's Irish Beef Stew.

Maggie was at the other end of the counter, rubbing a slab of bone-in beef chuck with a rub that she and Peter had created. She stopped and looked over at Millie, waiting for her to complete her thought as she had come to do with her best friend and boss. They had known each other for over five years now, and Millie had changed little, the beautiful head of white hair still trimmed a no-nonsense short, the cheeks a little fuller, but still with a rosy glow, and the stocky body emitting a force field of energy and strength.

Peter came to Empire Springs every other week or so and pitched in at the restaurant. He and Millie hit it off right from the start. The first time Peter arrived, he showed up in the middle of a busy lunch hour, threw on an apron, and took over the grill. He was a whiz at slapping a burger together with condiments, adding the sides; moving on to the next order, tossing fries in the fryer, assembling a club sandwich like a maestro, his fingers and hands moving with laser speed; and all of this done with the bon vivant demeanor of someone having the time of his life.

When the dust finally settled, Millie told Peter, "You can come and cook in my kitchen anytime, hon." The three of them were on the restaurant's back porch. Millie, sitting in the middle, motioned to the backyard garden, which was tilled over. "You like my eighty-eighty fallow field?"

Peter scrunched up his face into a question mark. He then brought his finger to his temple. "Eighty feet by eighty feet, right?"

She smiled her big-cheeked grin and threw a wink at Maggie. "Smart boy you got there, Maggie." Millie leaned into Peter, elbow nudging his side. "And plus it's nice to have a fellow round body in the kitchen."

A huge grin came over Peter's face. "My sentiments exactly, Millie."

Peter was not only a big hit with Millie but also with John. For John's fifth birthday, Peter bought him a peewee baseball mitt and baseball and would play catch with John in Millie's front yard.

Maggie hadn't considered Peter the athletic type, but he told her he had been a catcher in high school. "It's the position where fat kids go to die," he told her with a laugh. Peter ran John through fielding drills, showing him how to position himself—"Stay low to meet the ball, John." Peter would assume the fielding position, and John would drop his glove between his legs, his darling eyes alive with anticipation. It was as though John was experiencing an entirely new world, in not only baseball, but a relationship with an adult male—something in his life that had been missing. And the boy was a natural at the art of baseball. He had quick reflexes and a fluid throwing motion—he was his father's son. And in that regard, he had persisted in asking Maggie why he didn't have a daddy, "like all the kids in day care."

"It's complicated, honey," Maggie had replied. "When you are older, we will sit down, and I will explain."

John squinted a disappointed look at Maggie, and the eyes opened as if he had figured something out. "How old?" he said.

"Twelve," Maggie said.

"Twelve?" John said in a querulous tone. "That's too long, Mommy."

"Okay," Maggie said, "when you are ten, I will tell you all about it."

John squinted another querulous look at Maggie. "What's *it*?"

Maggie felt as though she was on the witness stand. Her son had his father's analytical mind. "I will tell you," Maggie said in a patient voice, "why you don't have a daddy here with you." She gave him a look—*Okay?*

John looked back at his mother, not completely satisfied, and then shrugged as if to say, "I'm a little boy; not much I can do."

When Peter did visit, he stayed in Daniel's bedroom downstairs. Maggie knew that Millie would not approve of her and Peter sharing a bed, with John in the same house. So, after a lunch rush, they would zip back over to Millie's house, race into Daniel's old room, tear each other's clothes off, and bang the living bejesus out of each other. Then they would quickly dress and haul ass back to Millie's Place. Peter always made a game out of it, checking his watch on departure and then when back in the kitchen. "New world record for a conjugal visit," he would say loud enough for Millie to hear, "twenty minutes and thirty-two seconds."

Millie once replied, "Round man move with lightning speed in kitchen," she said in a sotto voice à la Tonto, "and on way to make wampum with Maid Maggie." Millie then threw a bug-eyed look at Peter before the two of them broke out in hands-on-knees laughter.

But as much as Maggie was enjoying this magical part of her life, she had a watchful eye on the future: Peter had mentioned that he planned to move full-time to Portland no later than the end of the year to scout around for investors for the restaurant he wanted to open there.

"I figure I may have to get a job in a restaurant first, to get the lay of the land," he had told Maggie one recent evening on Millie's back patio. It was late September, and a full moon was out; behind them Millie's timber house was aglow in the moonlight; off in the distance, the faint warning barks of a dog sounded; the hills in the distance stood out black against a moody blue-black sky.

Maggie considered her relationship with Peter as more of a good friend, with whom she shared a passion for cooking and sexual gratification. Peter had sensed this from the beginning and had never tried to make it more than it was. But, Maggie knew, if she wanted, that Peter would marry her. It was nothing in what he said that tipped his hand, but more a fleeting glance of admiration, from time to time. In that look there was hope that she might come around and despair that she wouldn't.

"I'm going to ask you this," Peter said as he lifted a bottle of cabernet off the table and filled their glasses, "because if I don't, I will never forgive myself for not asking." Peter turned to Maggie.

Maggie was looking out at Millie's backyard, a swath of wild grass and wildflowers, reminding her of a field she used to play in as a child.

"Will you and John come to Portland with me?"

Maggie heard the lonesome, fading howl of the dog, its bark a gravelly whisper. It seemed so very far away now. She took Peter's hand in hers and leaned her head on his shoulder. "I wish I could say—"

"Say it then, Maggie," Peter cut in with a tone of urgency that Maggie had never heard from him before. "Say that you and John will travel with me to Portland to share our lives together." Peter raised his hand to ask for a moment.

"I fell in love with you the first moment I laid eyes on you, Maggie Meyers." He took a sip of his wine and flicked away a gnat buzzing about his face. "In that moment it was as though I knew you and all your secrets and dreams and even the scars of your past in that one moment that I wish I could hold for infinity."

Maggie wiped the tears streaking her cheek. "I am so sorry, Peter."

CHAPTER 30

After Peter left for Portland, Maggie was sick for two weeks. Not the kind of sickness that keeps you in bed, but a heartbreaking, indescribable weariness of body and soul. Part of her wanted to accept Peter's offer to move and start a new life with him in Portland. It would have been grand to keep a male influence in John's life, and also the excitement of being part of opening a new restaurant. Though she did love Peter, Maggie was not in love with him and never would be.

She adored him as a friend and fellow cook, but she had been in love with one man in this life, and that was the standard Maggie went by.

She had waited over a week to tell her son, fearful of John's reaction to losing his *Pete*. That's what John called Peter because he told his mother, "Peter is not a baseball player's name." He then lowered his brow and with a slant to his eyes said in a voice of someone much older, "Pete is a baseball name."

When Maggie finally told him that Peter had moved away, John had replied with a questioning glint, "For good, Mommy?"

John's spirit sagged for a few days, and then one evening when Maggie was tucking him into bed, his eyes drifted to a yellow toy biplane suspended on a wire from the ceiling; "Mommy ..." he said, shifting his gaze to three silhouette paintings of a bear, buck, and moose. He then looked directly at his mother. "Don't be sad anymore."

Maggie forced a smile and fussed with John's hair, which always reminded her of his father's. Even from a distance there was something to the striking blackness of the wavy hair that rippled in a sort of sideways slant.

John's eyes brightened as if an idea had come to him. "I promise not to miss Pete anymore if you do."

Maggie felt the tears welling in her eyes. "I promise," she said as she leaned forward and kissed her little boy good night.

CHAPTER 31

It was hard to believe that Maggie had been in Empire Springs for eleven years. As the years went by, John continued to inquire about his father. "How come my last name is different than yours, Mom?" John had asked when he was six. Maggie realized she needed to tell him some things, not everything, but enough. "You are named after your father, Johnny O'Brien." She went on to tell him that his father lived far away. "Can he come visit?"

"Maybe someday," Maggie said. She hated herself for being evasive, but … *It is what it is.*

Over the years, Maggie had stayed in contact with Nora, who had gotten married and had two kids. A few years back, Nora mentioned the Raw Bar had closed. "Bethesda is changing, Maggie—redevelopment." Nora's tone indicated, *Not good, but that's the way it is.* Her comments on Johnny were always the same. "He's dating here and there, but nothing serious."

Last time they spoke, Nora said that it seemed odd that Johnny had never gotten serious with a woman, "since you, Maggie—something doesn't add up."

Maggie realized that Johnny had never told anyone about his heart condition—so Johnny.

Recently, ten-year-old John had asked Maggie if he could call his father on the telephone. "No," Maggie said with meaning. "No phone calls." John started to speak, and Maggie raised her hand firmly. "No."

Millie had never interfered in any of this, only saying that if Maggie ever wanted to talk, she would listen. But for Maggie there was nothing to talk about. She could not, no, she would not, contact Johnny, and she would not allow her son to. She had spent more than a few sleepless nights running it all through her head. She was being selfish, she knew that. And maybe it was partly pride in Johnny turning her down all those years ago. He'd had his chance.

But it was more than that. Too many years had passed, and it would have thrown her internal world into turmoil. She just wasn't going to go down that path again—it was closed. She would be the best mother to John that she could be.

But tensions rose between mother and son, until finally Maggie and John sat down at the kitchen table.

She told John that his father had not wanted to marry her all those years ago, and it hurt her deeply.

"Does he know about me?" John asked.

Maggie felt her body tighten as though a cord had been yanked from head to toe. This was the moment she had dreaded. "No," she said.

"Not fair, Mom."

"No," Maggie said, "but that's the way it is."

"When I am old enough, I will find my dad," John said in a respectful but assured voice as though he was in the right.

"Fair enough," Maggie said, "but until then …"

After that, there was a grudging understanding from John. He didn't ask anymore about his father, but, at times, Maggie could sense him stewing about it, lying on the sofa, tossing a baseball into the air, over and over, a disgruntled look of someone thinking, *What if?*

As for cooking competitions, Maggie had been going to the Apple Autumn Festival every year in Gliberville, and last year she came in third for her Mexican chicken chili soup. But as much as she enjoyed it, it was the only competition she entered since she didn't like being away from John. "Once a year is enough," she told Millie, who had encouraged Maggie to enter other competitions.

Since Peter's departure over five years ago, Maggie's love life had been sporadic. She had a couple of flings with fellow cooks in Gliberville, each of which lasted a few months, Maggie ending it when they started to get serious.

Maggie still refused to consider going out with any of the local men. It seemed if she got involved, she knew herself well enough to know that she would eventually break it off. And then she would see him in town or at the restaurant with that heartbroken look.

She realized the effect she had on men who fell under her spell—it was like a superpower. Breaking up had been bad enough in a long-distance relationship, as with Peter. She couldn't imagine what it would be like in Empire Springs.

So Maggie resigned herself to long dry spells, but Millie had warned her, "Don't end up like me, all dried up and empty." They were on the back patio, after another long day at the restaurant, the sky aglitter in stars, a pale moon hung low in the sky spilling silver light on the inexorable hills. Millie took a sip of her sherry, and then let out a heavy sigh. "I've been with one man in my entire life, and after my husband's death, I could never …" She looked off for a moment and then back at Maggie. "A few fellas after a proper waiting period asked me out, but I wasn't ready to go through all that." She took another careful sip of her wine. "By the time I might have considered going out with the right guy," she said with a shrug, "it was too late. I never got asked out again."

CHAPTER 32

"What time is John's game, Maggie?" Millie asked. "Four," Maggie said as she added kale—a new ingredient— to a pot of her chicken tortilla soup.

Millie was scooping out balls of ground beef, with an ice cream scooper, onto a cutting board and patting them into patties. "I hear from Wilbur he's by far the best player on the team."

"Wilbur's great," Maggie said. "John loves playing for him."

"I want you to go to the game," Millie said as she continued to scoop and pat the ground meat.

"I can't leave you here on a Saturday with only Raymond and one waitress."

Millie shook her head and smiled as if mostly to herself. "If you think I would allow you to miss your son's first Little League baseball game ..." Millie gave Maggie her *you have got to kidding me* look.

Maggie made the drive over in her minivan—she finally got around to putting the woody in storage at Black Bart's Salvage a few years back. "I won't charge you any rent; looking at it every day is fair compensation," Black Bart told her, "and I'll drive it from time to time to keep the engine up to snuff."

John's baseball game was at the junior high school on the other side of the parkland that abutted the O'Connor estate. Maggie took a seat in the bleachers and said hello to a smattering of parents, most of whom she knew from the restaurant. There was a nervous energy in the stands, the voices a little louder and edgier, as if anticipating something that could be very good or possibly bad—these were their baby boys, after all, playing their first organized game of baseball.

John's team was the home team, and the game began with him at shortstop. Wilbur had told Maggie that he would also pitch. Maggie wasn't worried about John not playing well. Not only was he a good athlete, but he had an even-keel disposition that she thought would allow him to handle the inevitable errors and strikeouts.

As the game progressed, John not only made every play at shortstop, but he had three hits—his only out a scorching line drive to the third baseman—and pitched the last two innings to seal the win. During the game, some of the fathers commented on John's play. "He's a natural, Maggie." "What an arm and fluid pitching motion," another dad said.

The mothers, on the other hand, commented to Maggie about John's social skills. "Such good manners." Maggie had to smile at that one. That was Millie's doing. She was a stickler for *yes ma'am, no sir* to adults. "He is a pleasure to have around, such a spirit about him." That was what people had said about John's father.

On the way home, John asked, "Was my father a baseball player?" They were driving past the O'Connor estate. It was the first time he had brought up his father in over a year, since Maggie had said no phone calls.

Maggie pulled the car over to the side of the road. "He was a shortstop." She was startled as a large dark blue, four-door pickup truck stopped in the road. The power window lowered. It was Mr. O'Connor. "Everything all right?"

"Yes," Maggie said. "Having a little mother and son talk."

Mr. O'Connor flashed a brilliant smile, jutting his dimpled chin out the window for a closer look. He recognized John in his baseball uniform and said, "How'd the game go, son?"

John slid over next to Maggie and said out his mother's opened window. "Pretty good."

"Pretty good?" Mr. O'Connor said with an inquiring slant to his brow.

"He got three hits and pitched two scoreless innings to save the game," Maggie said as she wrapped her arm around John's shoulder.

"I believe we got us a ballplayer on our hands." Mr. O'Connor offered another glistening smile, followed by a wink at John as though they were old comrades, and raised his hand goodbye.

John slid over and out of his mother's embrace.

"I only saw your father play football, never baseball," Maggie said, "but his friends told me he was very good."

"Yeah," John said in a tone that indicated he'd like to hear more.

Part of Maggie wanted to end this conversation about Johnny, but she knew it was only fair to respond. She talked about watching Johnny O'Brien play high school football. "He was a quarterback, quick and decisive. I couldn't take my eyes off of him." Maggie's mind drifted back to the bleachers at Walter Johnson High School, a ninth-grader watching the senior star quarterback display his magic on the gridiron. "He was something else," Maggie said before she caught herself. But something had been let loose inside her, and there seemed no stopping it. "You are the spitting image of your father, John, the spitting image."

"You named me after him, right?" John said more as a conversational statement than a question since he already knew this fact.

"Yes," Maggie said, in a remembering voice, "Johnny O'Brien."

"It's a great baseball name," John said. "Isn't it, Mom?"

Maggie wiped her glistening eyes with the heels of her hands, removed a tissue out of her purse, and blew her nose. She took a breath and was about to speak.

"I know it upsets you to talk about him," John said. "But I still don't understand. Why can't I see him?"

"Okay, John, here's why."

Maggie told John the complete story about Johnny's heart condition and how there was a fifty-fifty chance his progeny could have inherited it, and that John had not; how Johnny, at now over forty, could die anytime; and how Johnny told Maggie that he wouldn't marry her, though she said she didn't care about his condition. "But he was adamant that it wouldn't be fair to me to be married to someone who could die so early in life and not have children."

John straightened in his seat and looked at Maggie with such utter sincerity. "I want more than your stories, Mom," John said in a soft voice, a voice much older than his years. It was not only his father's voice, but how he would have responded. "When I am old enough, I am going to find him."

"I know," Maggie said as she reached for John's hand and held it. "I wouldn't stop you from that, John," Maggie said. "But that's a few years down the road. Until then …" Maggie's voice drifted off, and she removed his ball cap and kissed John on the forehead. "Until then, let's put it on the back burner."

The morning following John's first Little League game, he told Maggie that he had a dream that he was playing catch with his father. "He looked like an older version of me, Mom." John told Maggie this at Millie's breakfast nook—which O'Connor Construction had built a few years back, Brent O'Connor only charging cost—with a view of the rising sun casting a stream of reddish-golden light that silhouetted the black hills. "And not only that, Mom," John said as he spread jam over his English muffin, "but he threw the ball like me." John cocked his arm in a throwing motion and followed through.

"Oh," Maggie said as she poured a glass of orange juice and set it in front of her son.

"The best part was his laugh," John said as he cradled his glass of juice and swished it around, creating an eddy of pulp on the surface. "It was magical." John took a swig of juice and said, "I didn't want the dream to end."

CHAPTER 33

By the time John was thirteen years old, he was pretty much up and running on his own. He made breakfast in the morning for Maggie and Millie, worked Saturdays as a busboy at Millie's Place, and arranged rides to all his various athletic practices, saving Maggie having to slip away from work.

"He's a go-getter just like my Daniel was at that age," Millie had commented to Maggie. "Cherish these last few years before he goes off into the world." They were on the back porch of the restaurant after the lunch rush. "The first eighteen years of Daniel's life, I saw him every day and took it for granted." Millie stared off for a moment as though seeing back then. "Now he's a ranger just like his dad, but Oregon is oh so far away."

Daniel's departure, first for college in Washington state and then after graduation moving to Oregon, had dampened Millie's spirit, which Maggie had always thought indefatigable. She still had that spark of life about her, but at times when they were alone, Maggie saw it in her eyes, a wistful remembering look. Maybe of not only Daniel but her husband, dead all these years—the family that could have been.

Maggie and Millie were in the same boat, paddling against the strong current of time, both with sons without a father around, and both adoring their only child.

"He's all I got left in this life," Millie had told Maggie, as they stood in the driveway the day Daniel drove off for Oregon, his car crammed with all of his cherished possessions. Maggie put her arm around Millie's shoulder. "You raised a fine son into manhood, Millie."

Millie was holding Daniel's letterman sweater, which she had asked him to leave as a keepsake. She looked at Maggie and crinkled a smile. "You right, hon, mama bear has to let her little boy go." She brought his sweater to her nose and breathed in his boyhood scent.

"And," Maggie said with emphasis, "you should be proud of the son you have raised." Maggie laughed and smiled big at Millie. "Remember to repeat those words to me when John goes off into the world."

Though John hadn't gone away yet, Maggie was seeing less and less of him as sports began to take a bigger chunk of his life: peewee football in the fall, basketball in the winter, and, of course, baseball in the summer. John was a big hit with the parents who carpooled the boys to practices. "He's such a good kid," one father told Maggie at the restaurant, "and a solid influence on my boy." The father offered Maggie a nod of conviction. "He's just a joy to be in the company of."

Maggie wished she could take the credit for John turning out the way he did, but she realized it was a team effort between her, Millie, and the day-care woman she had taken him to for the first eleven years of his life. And of course there was also the genetics involved—John was his father's son.

By John's senior year of high school, he was a three-sport star: quarterback in football, guard in basketball, and, of course, shortstop in baseball—his favorite sport. He had worked the last two summers for O'Connor Construction, first as a carpenter's assistant on a renovation of a mansion a couple of towns north of Empire Springs, and then as Mr. O'Connor's gofer. He drove around in a company pickup from job site to job site delivering materials, and on Fridays he delivered paychecks.

Maggie heard from more than one of the regulars from O'Connor Construction, "What a great kid you got there, Maggie."

A group of them had been coming in for years every Friday after work and sat at the bar, which Millie had renovated and expanded with a brass rail, stained glass mirror, and high-back swivel stools with leather cushions. "There's money in booze," Millie told Maggie. These men had worked for Brent O'Connor for years, an older group of men, who came in and drank their beers in quiet conversation. They talked sports mostly, and Maggie's son was now a major topic of conversation. "The O'Brien boy is as fine a dual threat quarterback as ES High has ever had," one man told Wilbur, who still tended the bar. Another one added, "And he's as smart as a whip. Picked things up that summer he worked on my crew like he'd been doing it all his life."

Maggie loved hearing Wilbur repeat these compliments to her. And, of course, Wilbur always had his own comments to add: "All around good boy, Maggie. Yes, indeed."

And Mr. O'Connor had taken an interest in John. He was a regular attendee at John's games, and even had him over to his house to offer a few pointers on quarterbacking.

John told Maggie that Mr. O'Connor had been a quarterback at Empire Springs "back in the dark ages," and the only thing that worried him about John was that John was going to break all of his records.

Brent O'Connor was the main man in Empire Springs. He owned many of the buildings in town, including Millie's Place. Millie told Maggie that he was a good and generous man, but, "Like I've said before, you don't ever want to cross Brent O'Connor. He's runs his company and this town like a benevolent emperor."

And this being senior year, John would soon be applying to college, something Maggie dreaded to think about, not having her boy around. John was an excellent student, and scored very high on his SAT exam in both math and English.

"Combine his high academics," the guidance counselor had told Maggie, "with his athletic prowess, and he can get into just about any school he wants."

Though Maggie had been saving money ever since she left Mexico, she didn't have the resources to pay for something like an Ivy League school. She had talked to Black Bart about the value of the woody, and he said it was now worth twenty thousand—*Thank you very much, Peter, for the good advice.*

But that was not nearly enough to cover even one year at a really fine college. Wilbur had told her that John might get some financial aid to play baseball if he had a good year coming up. "But," he added, "baseball is his best bet because 170 soaking wet ain't hardly big enough for big-time football."

Worse case was that John could go to a community college and then apply for student loans to finish at a four-year school. But Maggie had an inkling that there was going to be someone to come to John's aid when all was said and done. John had mentioned that Mr. O'Connor had talked to him about his alma mater—the University of Pennsylvania—and said it was the greatest experience of his life. Part of Maggie hated to think of John going that far away, but the other part, which wanted what was best, overruled.

1996, Maggie thought, *is going to be a turning point year for John … and me.*

CHAPTER 34

A sudden swirl of wind ruffled the American flag at the far end of the Empire Springs High football field. The air was cool and crisp, and it reminded Maggie of sitting in the stands at WJ, all those years ago, watching Johnny O'Brien perform his magic.

It was the fifth game of the season, and the Empire Springs Eagles were undefeated. John was having a standout season leading the team from his quarterback position, all five feet eleven, 170 pounds of him.

But this game today didn't come without some sacrifice on Maggie's part. It was also the weekend of the Autumn Apple Festival in Gliberville. John and Millie had tried to convince Maggie to attend and skip the game, but she would have none of it. "What," she had said, "and miss the biggest game of the year? No way."

Maggie had put on a brave front in that regard, but it was only for one year, and there was always next year's festival. But there would be no more next year for watching John play ball.

The Eagles were playing their biggest rival, the Central High Lions, also undefeated. The stands were packed for the game, including Brent and Katie O'Connor sitting on both sides of Maggie. Of course, Millie couldn't attend, having to work at the restaurant. So it was Maggie and the O'Connors sitting in a cluster of parents of other Empire Springs players, all excited and raring to go. "Johnny's got to keep an eye out for that middle linebacker, number 52, Butch Cadell," one father said, looking over his shoulder at Maggie. "He's gonna follow him wherever he goes."

John was now called Johnny by all his friends and their parents. John had initiated it during his first Little League season, telling his buddies that Johnny O'Brien was a ball player's name. And soon it stuck. Maggie and Millie were about the only two left still calling him John.

Maggie wanted to keep a clear divide between father and son. And Millie seemed to pick up on this and continued to call him John. And, of course, John seemed to understand the reason his mother and Millie didn't call him Johnny. "You two have called me one name all my life," he told Maggie a few years back, as the two of them took a break on the back porch of the restaurant. "Sides, it'd seem funny you and Millie calling me Johnny."

John's dreams of his father occurred a few times a year, and it was the same scenario: the two of them playing catch, and his father calling him Johnny Junior. "They always seem so real, Mom, and kind of mysteriously magical at the same time."

Maggie found these dreams disconcerting and would only say, "Had another one, huh?" She would then nod, look off for a moment, and then go on about her business.

The game was a seesaw battle right from the start, and the father in the stands had been right about number 52 following John everywhere he went. On one bruising tackle, the boy blindsided John, who was avoiding other tacklers, and lifted him off the ground and drove him hard into the turf, landing on top of him. Maggie held her breath before John bounced up and ran back to the huddle.

"Johnny has to be aware of 52 at all times," Mr. O'Connor said as general conversation. And after that, John was on the lookout for Butch Cadell, who was a big kid with good athletic instincts. He seemed to have a nose for the football and was making tackles from sideline to sideline. But John was the quickest player on the field, and he used this to his advantage, juking and faking out would-be tacklers, including 52.

Just like his dad, John moved on the field like lightning in a bottle. And much like the first time Maggie saw Johnny O'Brien play football, John won the game with a last-second zigzagging run for a touchdown. The stands erupted with wild cheers, and more than few parents beamed huge smiles at Maggie. "What a run," Mr. O'Connor said.

"He reminds me of you, Brent," Mrs. O'Connor said, loud enough for others to hear.

Brent O'Connor raised his brow as though considering and then glinted a smile. It was a proud smile, a paternal smile of seeing a glimmer of his past in a boy on the same field he starred on all those years ago.

After the game, a group of parents and a few of the players went to Millie's Place to celebrate the big win. By the time Maggie and John got there, every seat was taken. They went into the kitchen and found Millie and Raymond dishing out platters of the Saturday dinner special, Maya's Mexican Beef Stew, which Maggie had tinkered with over the years.

Millie glanced over at mother and son, wiped her hands on her apron and said, "Heard all about the big win—congrats, John."

Meanwhile, Maggie was tying on an apron and made a beeline toward the stove. "Ray—mooond," she said in stretching out the name, "Maggie to the rescue."

"Hah," Raymond hooted, "in the nick of time, Magg—eee." He was tending to burgers on the grill, his ponytail now snow white, his long, large body had increased in the belly à la Santa Claus, but he could still "slide and glide," in the kitchen, moving about with effortless ease from cook to bottle washer to busboy.

John, now in an apron, went to the double sink and began dousing dirty dishes in soapy water and then spraying them clean in the second sink.

"How 'bout that," Raymond said, in an exaggerated tone, "Johnny Football to the rescue."

During the cocktail hour, Brent O'Connor held court with some of the older men at the bar. "Johnny ... O'Brien ..." Brent said as he raised his hand as though getting ready to take oath, "not only a team player, but ..." He paused for a moment as Maggie was within earshot taking an order from Wilbur at the bar. Brent's expression shifted from every pore of his being exuding bon vivant from the wide, toothy smile and eyes alive with anticipation to a more serious demeanor, the eyes suddenly lowered to half-mast, the smile now a thoughtful crease of the lips. "Your boy, Maggie, is something special. Yes indeed," he said as the eyes once again grew wide and lips parted into that patented O'Connor smile.

After-hours at the restaurant, Maggie, Johnny, Raymond, and Millie sat at the round table with Brent and Katie O'Connor. The infectious mood, a spirited happiness, was powered by the forceful personality of Brent O'Connor, who reminisced about his high school days. "Back then folks didn't have two nickels to rub together but," he said clasping his hands together, "we were a tight community and helped each other out whenever we could." He shrugged and then turned his gaze on John. "I was accepted to attend the University of Pennsylvania on a partial academic scholarship but didn't have the necessary funds."

John sat there with keen-eyed alertness, as though opportunity was knocking. "Really?" John said.

Mr. O'Connor went on to talk about the womenfolk having bake sales, the men cutting back on cigarettes and liquor and donating the extra money to the "Get Brent to Penn" campaign. "We were still short until an anonymous donor chipped in the rest."

Sunday morning after the big game, Maggie was in the kitchen doing breakfast dishes, John in his room studying, and Millie napping on the sofa. The kitchen phone rang, and Maggie answered it quickly before it woke Millie.

"Maggie, Brent O'Connor, here. I have a proposition for you and your son."

One hour later, Maggie and John pulled into the long driveway to the O'Connor estate. John had been in the house over the course of working the last two summers for the construction company, and Maggie for Christmas parties the last two years, which made her feel like she was *really* part of the community, though she sensed that being John's mother had something to do with it. It was considered a big deal in town to get an invite.

Mr. O'Connor was waiting in front of the double mahogany front doors, with sidelights and transoms. He had aged well over the years Maggie had known him. The face had a few creases at the corners of the eyes, but still he had that handsome athletic look, and the gray hair, tinged white, was full, and he had maintained the upright carriage and stance of a strong, confident man. He raised his hand in greeting and welcomed Maggie in with a nod and John a pat on the back. "Come on in," he said as he opened the door.

The foyer floor was made of earth-tone stones and was complemented by white bead-board walls adorned with electric candlelight sconces, redwood-framed mirror, and small paintings of pastoral scenes. A staircase, with iron balusters and newels, curved gently to the second floor. The house reeked of understated class.

Mr. O'Connor led Maggie and John through a hallway, a massive kitchen on their left with granite countertops and shiny appliances, into a library-office off the living room.

"Please, sit," Mr. O'Connor said as he offered his hand to a leather sofa situated in front of a massive glass-enclosed walnut bookshelf.

Mr. O'Connor moved a wing chair from the corner of the sofa and placed it across a coffee table, facing his guests. He asked if they would like anything to drink, and both declined as an expectant air of tension fell over the room. He leaned forward in the chair, forearms on thighs, hands clasped. "What I would like to propose is a game plan for Johnny's future."

CHAPTER 35

"What'd you think, Mom?"

Maggie looked out the car window, the O'Connor estate on her left, fading from view. "It's very generous." Maggie glanced at John, then back on the road, as a park ranger in a pickup approached, hand raised hello. Maggie returned a wave and said, "Penn is an Ivy League school." She felt her heart sink to her stomach. But she didn't want her emotions to sway John's decision. "I'm with you on whatever you decide."

Of course, a free education at a top-notch school was not something John decided to pass up. How could he?

By February, John received his acceptance letter and called Mr. O'Connor with the news. "Great news, son, great news." He then offered to fly John in his private jet to Philadelphia during the upcoming summer, where, "I am meeting some old college chums on the weekend of the Fourth of July and would like to give you a tour of the school."

John told Maggie about the offer and also a side trip he wanted to take. "I checked the train schedule from Philly to Washington, DC, and it's less than two hours. I want to meet my father."

Maggie knew this day would come, but it was none the easier as worlds were on a crash course. She started to tell John where his father last lived when he interrupted. "I have an address and phone number for a John O'Brien on Hempstead Street in Bethesda, Maryland."

"How?" Maggie said as she felt a quiver in her voice.

"I called long-distance information, and they gave it to me." John went on to say that, no, he hadn't called the number and wouldn't. "I want to go by and see what's what, before I give myself away." John lifted his shoulders and scrunched up his face. "In case I see ..." He paused and cleared his throat. "Anyway that's my plan."

And while John's life was tracking forward with great promise, Maggie's had hit a rut. She was now in her late forties and, though still attractive, she had lost that youthful glow. Men still offered an admiring glance from time to time, but they no longer gave the look of someone having discovered a great find, like the first time Peter saw her at the B&B in Gliberville, but rather a look of interested appraisal. She hadn't been with a man in over five years, since her last short-lived relationship with a fellow cook at the Autumn Apple Festival. A been-there-done-that common thread ran through her life: preparing the specials each day, burgers and fries, simple dishes for simple folk. She knew Millie wouldn't go for any exotic recipes that she read about in *Bon Appétit,* such as duck breast with mustard greens or fregola with green peas, mint, and ricotta. And then there was John going off to school three thousand miles away, and she didn't even want to think about him meeting his father.

So that spring, Maggie decided to ask for some time off, not only from work but her life in Empire Springs, something she hadn't done in eighteen years as an employee or resident.

Maggie decided to drive the minivan—which in six years only had thirty thousand miles on it—to Taos, over eight hundred miles, through the desert with its stark landscape and heat. It was a climate she had not been in since Mexico. And Millie and John were all for it. "You deserve it, Mom," John said. "About time," Millie said. "Lord knows you've earned it."

The first day on the road, Maggie drove five hundred miles due east, stopping in Flagstaff. She had brought along a sleeping bag, and after dinner at a diner, she decided to drive off the highway onto the hardpan high desert.

She realized she was trying to regain a portion of her youth by doing this, but so what. The ground was a bit bumpy, but Maggie rattled along a ways off the highway, coming to a stop at the base of an ocher-hued butte. It was dusk, the sun painting the landscape in a swath of earthy tones. The only sound she heard was the faint howl of a coyote. It was the first time she had heard that sound since that horrible night at the ranch, buck naked in the apple orchard, watching streams of smoke rise high into the night sky as the Night Ghosts burned El Rancho to the ground.

She locked the doors, pushed back the backseat, and unfurled her sleeping bag, first time since El Rancho. Darkness came on the land quickly, and with it, the coyote's howl fell silent. Lying on her back, Maggie could see through the back window the first hint of stars emerging.

In college, Maggie had taken an astronomy course as an elective and remembered that the stars in the night sky were images from a long, long time ago, like ghosts from another world. She felt as though she had transported herself to another world, in the middle of nowhere, a middle-aged woman alone in the back of a vehicle in search of what? Some ghostly remnant of her past?

Also, Maggie realized that this trip was a way to get off on her own and consider what the future held for her. Her son would soon be traveling east to begin on his life's journey and also seek out his father. What if John meets Johnny, and he is distant and curt—no, Johnny would never. But what if they bond—then what? Where did Maggie fit in? And would Johnny get upset with Maggie that he had never known about John, and could he turn John against her?

Maggie rolled over on her side and snuggled herself tight in her sleeping bag. *Did what I thought was right,* she told herself. As the fatigue from driving all day began to overcome her, Maggie thought that she would enjoy this trip and worry about the future in the future.

At dawn, Maggie woke with a start in the middle of a nightmare. John and Johnny were playing catch in the front yard of El Rancho, as Night Ghosts galloped down the dirt road. Father and son tried to run for it, but they were lassoed and dragged facedown to the front of the house where the ugly Charo awaited. "Well," Charo said, "if it isn't the sexy bitch's boys from Bethesda." Charo let out a bloodcurdling laugh and said, "We have fun now." He drew his knife from its sheath and put his boot on Johnny's throat. Fortunately for Maggie, she woke before the nightmare went any further.

She felt her heart racing. She sat up and took a deep breath. She exhaled and could see a vaporous stream of her breath. There was a chill in the air. A road sign not far from where she had turned off onto the desert had indicated an elevation of seven thousand feet. *No wonder it's cold,* Maggie thought as she got out of the car, in her bare feet, and stretched her hands overhead.

The desert was awakening with *cheek, cheek* and *birdie, birdie* calls of morning birds hiding in the shrubs and cacti of the scrubby land. The sun had risen, and though the air had a chill, it held a promise of warmth. "New day," Maggie said aloud. "Taos, here I come."

CHAPTER 36

B y early afternoon, Maggie found an RV park on the outskirts of Taos equipped with a bathroom and shower facilities. She could have gone to a motel, but something that she couldn't put a name to told her to rough it a bit. After a shower and change of clothes, Maggie drove into town for a quick walkabout and to inquire about some of the Indian pueblos she planned to visit tomorrow.

Walking about Taos, Maggie noticed the range in age of the people from early twenties to one woman well into her eighties who was inspecting paintings in the front window of an art gallery. She was impeccably dressed in a baby-blue turtleneck cashmere sweater, dark blue tailored jacket, and dark dress pants. She had the look of a wealthy art patron. There were other well-dressed folks here and there, but for the most part it was your run-of-the mill tourists, and of course the artists, who were easy to pick out.

They had an air about them of independence, of going their own way in this life, consequences be damned: Many of the men artists were in jeans and wore their graying hair in ponytails à la Raymond, and the women, some wearing turquoise bracelets and necklaces, were mostly in T-shirts and cutoffs. There was somberness about them as though life hadn't quite turned out the way they had expected. Maggie overheard a woman outside an art studio say, "Our work is not as important as it used to be, at least here in Taos." It seemed that many of the residents of this artsy town had seen better days.

Taos proper was a well-maintained stretch of adobe and stucco buildings with trees here and there. It had a Southwest flair to it, but with an affluence that she hadn't expected. There was the Hotel La Fonda, a grand old structure in faded mauve adobe, and upscale shops. Maggie had always envisioned Taos as a sort of funky down-and-out old western town that the artist community discovered and reveled in its disrepair.

Maggie had paid the proprietor of the RV park for two nights, not sure what her plans were. One thing she was certain of was to smoke one of the four fat doobies Raymond had given her. "Take a trip down memory lane," he told her. Maggie hadn't smoked marijuana in years, since Rack.

Back at the RV park, Maggie removed a beach folding chair from the car. There was one other vehicle in her row, a dinged and dented RV van with a shell on top. The sun was setting over Taos Mountain, a black outline cast against the russet-streaked sky. Maggie lit the joint and took a deep toke. She coughed and cleared her throat.

"Howdy."

Maggie turned to see a man dressed in flannel and jeans standing behind her, holding a six-pack of beer in one hand and a chair in the other. He was late thirties, a head of blondish-red hair, a two-day growth of stubble the same color as his hair, and a chiseled, ruddy look of someone who spent time outdoors.

"Hi, there," Maggie said as she offered her hand for him to join her.

The man unfolded his chair, sat, and pulled two beers off the plastic ring. "Care for a cold one?"

His name was Jack Brower, and he was a geologist on sabbatical from the University of New Mexico. They shared Maggie's joint over beers. Jack had been "taking walkabouts over this petrologically and volcanologically diverse land every chance I can get." He threw an *I can't help myself* smile at Maggie and said, "I am fascinated by rocks."

They exchanged looks.

"Okay," Jack said as he cracked open two more beers, "what's your excuse for being here?"

A tranquility had come over Maggie, a down-to-the-bone calmness, not only from the marijuana and beer but Jack's company. He was a guy comfortable in his own skin, who seemed to have found his calling in this life. "Reassessment," Maggie said.

"Ah," Jack said, "you've come to the right place."

They shared another joint, drank some more beer and small talked on the periphery of their personal lives. "I've wanted to be a geologist since I started a rock collection in the second grade."

Maggie glossed over her life in Empire Springs before letting slip, "I have an eighteen-year-old son who wants to meet his father for the first time."

"I never knew my father," Jack said in a changed voice, a vulnerable voice. "My mother wanted a child but not a husband." He went on to tell how his mother had lived in a commune before "it was in, and picked out an unsuspecting sperm donor." Jack shrugged and said, "She left the commune and made a life for herself and her son."

Jack raised his hands in front of him. "Everybody's got regrets." He then smiled at Maggie, a smile of admiration, a smile she hadn't seen in a while.

Maggie woke in the bunk space in the top shell of Jack's RV. There was something very reassuring about a girl's place in the universe, when lying naked next to a hunky guy also wearing his birthday suit. The sex last night and into the morning had done wonders. Jack had a hard body and used it with an amorous gusto that left Maggie gasping with carnal delight.

And he made her feel wanted and desired: "Not only do you look good," Jake told her, his arm wrapped around the back of her neck as they lay on their backs, the dawn light overhead through the glass top, "but you smell good too." He nuzzled his face into Maggie's hair. "I bet you've broken some hearts along the way."

CHAPTER 37

Jack took Maggie in and around Taos, dropping in and out of the craft shops, eating fry bread and Indian tacos at a food trailer off the highway—all made from scratch and delicious by an Indian couple that owned the business—and driving to a couple of Indian pueblo villages that Maggie found fascinating: the first had adobe houses built very close together and stacked two or three stories high. There was an edge of poverty about these Native American people, the men in jeans and denim shirts, the women in more traditional breechcloth with leather leggings and moccasins, selling jewelry and craftwork. There was something in their gaze that reminded Maggie of the hired hands at El Rancho, a look of displacement, a look that said this is not who we should be.

The second pueblo was smaller than the first. It was located in a mountain hamlet with a small Catholic church, with a pit of adobe-colored dirt that was reputed to possess the power to cure. The people of this village also appeared to live at a poverty level, but there wasn't the dispirited aura hanging over them as at the first pueblo. The men had more of a bounce to their step and a look of pride as though living in a village of providence.

That evening after visiting the pueblos, Jack took Maggie out to dinner at a Mexican restaurant two miles outside of Taos proper. It was run by a Mexican family in a house where the downstairs had been converted into two dining rooms, with the upstairs steps separating them.

The interior was simple yet elegant, with hardwood floors, white tablecloths, Indian artwork hanging on the muted-yellow walls. They sat at a corner table as the waitress—who Maggie guessed was the daughter by her youth and similar bone structure and demeanor of her placid brown face to the owner-hostess—brought a carafe of red wine. Jack poured out two glasses and raised his. "A toast," he said.

They clinked glasses, and Maggie said, "What are we toasting?"

"To a special time with a special woman." There was a tone of finality in his voice.

"We still have this evening," Maggie said with an arch of her brow, a knowing, confident smile firmly in place.

"Thank you for clearing that up," Jack said. He cleared his throat and said, "You were very quiet today at the pueblos."

Maggie took a sip of her wine. "Seeing how those people lived made me appreciate my life."

The waitress came by and asked if they needed anything. "We'll order in a bit," Jack said, nodding a thank-you. He looked over at Maggie for her to continue.

"I've had an unusual life, a different life," Maggie said. She looked up as a busboy whizzed by holding a tray of dirty dishes over his shoulder.

They were silent for a moment, before Maggie continued. "I've lost the great love of my life, dodged death, and had a son who is the spitting image of his father—my great love—who he now wants to meet for the first time." She looked off for a moment and then said, "I would not have traded any of it for anything."

Maggie took another sip of her wine and looked across the table at Jack. His square chin tucked into the sturdy neck, the gray eyes steady as you go, the lips fluttering around a knowing smile. "*And*," Maggie said, "for whatever obstacles I may encounter in the future, for that I am thankful."

Maggie knew she would never see Jack again: he lived over eight hundred miles from Empire Springs, and she was not looking for a long-distance relationship. The fact of the matter was that Maggie was not looking for any sort of relationship presently. She had too many things going on in her life with John soon to leave for college and planning to track down Johnny. The last thing Maggie needed was getting involved with a man, even one as good as Jack.

CHAPTER 38

The Fourth of July was on a Thursday. That Tuesday, Maggie drove John to the O'Connor estate. Mrs. O'Connor greeted mother and son at the front door and escorted them to the back patio, where they saw a sleek silver jet parked on the one-mile-long landing strip that ran parallel to the hills in the distance and cut through a meadow of wildflowers and scrub trees. A man in a pilot's uniform inspected the wings and tail, bending down and checking the landing gear. He was taking his time, like his boss, a thoughtful, confident man.

Way off to her left was Raymond's yurt, which he had now lived in for going on twenty years. It looked so small and vulnerable, as though she could extend her thumb and rub it away.

"Well, are we all ready?"

Maggie turned to the distinct voice of Mr. O'Connor. It was still a powerful, melodious voice. He was pulling a leather suitcase on rollers and was dressed in slacks and a polo shirt. A pair of aviation glasses propped up on his mane of silver-gray hair. From the first time Maggie saw him her first night in Empire Springs to this very moment, he exuded success—American success.

"Maggie," Mr. O'Connor said, "how about a quick tour of the aircraft before we take off."

"I'd like that." Of course, what she would really like was for none of this to be occurring. That John wasn't flying off to Philadelphia to tour the university all those miles away. That John wasn't taking the train down to DC and then making his way to Bethesda and Johnny's street. The thought of it made her nearly dizzy.

The inside of the plane had eight seats—two rows of two on each side of the aisle. The cockpit had two seats. "I'll fly some of the trip," Mr. O'Connor said as he motioned to one of the steering wheels attached to the gray metallic dashboard with an array of instrument panels.

Maggie hugged John inside the plane. She started to speak and felt a catch in her throat.

"I'll look after your boy, Maggie," Mr. O'Connor said. "Not to worry."

Maggie and Mrs. O'Connor watched the plane take off from the patio. It was like a silver arrow rising into the blue sky, gaining altitude and growing smaller and smaller, until she could no longer see it.

CHAPTER 39

John wouldn't return until late Sunday afternoon, and for the time he was gone, Maggie tried her damndest not to dwell on all the possibilities. Of course, she failed at it miserably. Even working in the kitchen at Millie's Place, where Maggie could normally lose herself in the task at hand, she could not stop thinking about John finding his father.

His schedule was to meet Mr. O'Connor's college chums on Wednesday. "Like everyone else he's ever met, John will be a big hit with my friends," Mr. O'Connor had told Maggie, on the phone the night before departure. "After he graduates, they can be a big help in helping him find a job."

Maggie felt as though she were losing a part of her son. Not that she didn't appreciate what Mr. O'Connor was doing, but it was never going to be the same.

On Thursday, an orientation tour of the college campus, and then, on Friday, John was taking the train to find his father. Mr. O'Connor had volunteered to go with him, but John said he needed to do this on his own.

Though the restaurant was only open for lunch on the Fourth, Maggie got to work at the crack of dawn—leaving a note for Millie that she had gone in early—and worked like a dervish chopping vegetables for salads and soups, and preparing burger patties. By the time Millie and Raymond arrived at nine in the morning, there was little left for them to do. It was now noon back east, and John's train was scheduled to arrive in Washington, DC, and from there Hempstead Street in Bethesda.

Maggie went out on the back porch and plopped down in a chair, as a weariness came over her. It was an edgy, bone tiredness that seemed to sap not only her energy but her ability to think clearly.

Millie came out and sat next to Maggie. She placed her hand on Maggie's and said, "Hang in there, hon."

Maggie sighed so heavily that it felt as though she had broken something loose inside her. "Hanging by a thread," she said. Maggie looked at Millie, who offered a what-the-heck shrug. "It's just not knowing what is going to happen."

"You're a fearless woman, Maggie," Millie said with a pat on Maggie's hand. "Whatever happens, you will be able to handle it." Millie gave Maggie a hard, confident look. "Remember what you told me about raising a fine son when Daniel left home for good?"

"Yes, I do," Maggie said as an old saying that she hadn't thought of in years rose in her mind: *Whatever will be, will be.*

CHAPTER 40

By six Sunday evening, Maggie heard the sound of a heavy car engine pull into the driveway. She peeked out the blinds and saw John get his bag from the back of Mr. O'Connor's trunk and make his way to the house.

They sat at the kitchen table, Maggie and John. Millie had left earlier for a friend's house—"Give you two some privacy and space to talk things out."

Maggie felt as though her head might explode, as she had a hundred questions to ask. John's expression was noncommittal, the eyes steady and sure, the lips sealed shut, the jaw jutting out just a tad—he called it his *game face*.

"Well?" Maggie said.

"Let me start from the beginning of the trip. The plane ride was a blast. I even got to sit in the cockpit," John said with a lift in his voice. "Philadelphia is a really neat city, and I had dinner with the men of clout, as Mr. O'Connor called them." He went on to say the university was even more than he had expected. "The campus is on the west side of town, beautiful stone architecture that makes you feel like you are in a special place."

Maggie was listening and not listening, as she kept wishing for John to get to the heart of the matter.

And then it came. "On Friday morning, I took the train from Philadelphia to Washington." John smiled as if mostly to himself. "I sat in custom class; Mr. O'Connor insisted on paying."

Maggie forced a weak smile, her heart in her stomach. "That was nice of him."

The smile left John's face, and in its place was a shadow of disappointment in his gaze. "From Union Station, I took a subway into Bethesda and then a bus. I walked a few blocks to Hempstead Street in Bethesda—really neat neighborhood." His tone was now that of strained observer.

"I stopped at an open space—Ayrlawn Rec Center, a sign read. There was a Fourth of July picnic going on, and something told me I would find what I was searching for."

John paused for a moment as if to collect himself. Maggie was looking closely at her son's face, searching for a hint of what was to come next, her mind racing with apprehension.

"There were nearly a hundred people of all ages from little kids to people the O'Connors' age. There was an energy to this gathering, a vibration of happiness that I felt as I observed from a safe distance behind a line of bushes, where I pulled my ball cap down low over my eyes and watched." John exhaled a stream of air. "And then I saw him."

Mother and son exchanged looks, and in that moment Maggie saw what she had feared.

"He looked like me," John said, "but older, just like in my dreams." John lifted a brow, his eyes saying, "Can you believe it?"

"He was standing with a group of men, big guys that looked like they could still play ball."

John leaned back in his chair and looked off for a moment and then turned his gaze back to his mother. And in her son's gaze, Maggie saw a mixture of reverence and sadness.

"It was like watching myself thirty years down the road," John said with a shrug. "I've never seen anyone with such ..."

"I have," Maggie said as she reached across the kitchen table and took John's hand in hers.

John shrugged again and told Maggie that later on Johnny played catch with a boy about eleven years old. "It was so like my dream of playing catch with him." John shook his head at the memory. "It was surreal, Mom. It really was."

He went on to tell about how Johnny threw the ball just like in the dream, and with the same facial expressions. "He had a perpetual smile on his face that seemed to light up everyone around him."

John then said how he was getting ready to go down and introduce himself when they stopped playing catch, and Johnny and the boy went over to a very attractive woman and a little girl around eight.

Maggie tried not to show any emotion, sitting so very still that she could feel her heart tapping in rhythm in her chest—*pit-a-pat-pit-a-pat.*

"I didn't see a ring on his finger," John said, "but the woman had a wedding band on hers." John paused and took a breath. "They sure acted like a family. He picked the little girl up and raised her high over his head. I couldn't tell what they were saying, but their actions spoke very clearly—I felt like an intruder."

Maggie didn't want to tell John that she knew if Johnny had gotten married, Nora would have called her. She felt a conflux of emotions: hurt that Johnny was involved with a woman and her family, hurt that he had rejected her, but most of all the hurt she now saw clearly in her son's eyes.

"I was back in Philly before dark."

Later that day, after John had gone out to a friend's house, Maggie called Nora. They hadn't spoken in over a year, but Nora had always understood why she called—she understood what Johnny had meant to her.

"Nora," Maggie said as she answered the phone.

"I knew you would call," Nora said. She went on to explain that she had attended Johnny's annual Fourth of July picnic down at Ayrlawn Rec Center. "I was late, and on my way to the field, I saw a young guy wearing a ball cap crouching in some bushes, watching the picnic." After a beat, Nora said, "He was a dead ringer for Johnny when he was younger."

There was a silent pause before Nora said, "Is that your and Johnny's son?"

"Yes." Maggie's said in a raspy whisper. "Nora, I ahh—"

"Maggie, you don't have to explain anything to me."

"It's complicated, Nora."

"You know I won't say anything."

169

Maggie asked about the woman and two children John saw Johnny with at the picnic.

"Maybe forty, widowed, from Wisconsin, and pretty, very pretty," Nora said in her matter-of-fact tone. "First serious woman in his life since you, Maggie. Rumor has it he might marry her and adopt the children." There was silence on the line before Nora added, "I don't believe it. Do you?"

There was another pause before Maggie said. "I am happy for Johnny."

"She lives just a few blocks from Johnny's house, and Danny McKenzie tells me he is over there all the time."

After Maggie hung up the phone, she felt as though she might faint before her stomach churned something terrible. It seemed the world she had built around herself, an illusionary world, was crashing all around her.

PART 3

Full Circle

CHAPTER 41

2007

Maggie found out about Johnny's death by chance. She had recently gotten an online account to read the *Washington Post* and happened to peruse the obituary page when one death notice caught her eye:

John (Johnny) O'Brien, owner and operator of O'Brien's Landscape Company, died on September 28 of cardiac arrest.

Visitation will be held at Pumphrey's Funeral Home in Bethesda, Maryland, on Tuesday October 2 ...

There was nothing in the obit about surviving relatives or a wife and children. Maggie thought about calling Nora, but she had not spoken to her since the phone call about the picnic. It had been years. And what was the purpose. Johnny was dead. Maggie had actually gone through a grieving process when Nora had told her about the pretty widow at the picnic with the two young children. At that moment it seemed as though she had been in love with a myth more than a man. And over the years a figurative scar tissue formed in her heart in regard to Johnny. And though his memory still festered at times as the years went by, she told herself that she still had their son in her life, the son Johnny O'Brien never knew existed.

Maggie called John in Philadelphia and broke the news.

"Oh," was all John could say. After he'd had seen his father at the picnic with the young family, he told Maggie, "A little something died inside of me when I saw him with those two kids. I felt like I would have ruined his happiness, accidental ghost from his past."

After that, John didn't mention his father, except to query Maggie the first few years after as to whether he should still meet his dad. "That's something only you can decide," was Maggie's patented reply.

Maggie then told John that there was no mention of a family in the obit.

"But I thought—"

"That's right, John," Maggie said. "You thought, not knew."

"And I could have …"

"John, don't beat yourself up over this. I've done enough of that over the years for the two of us."

As Maggie hung up the phone, Millie came in from the sliding glass door to the kitchen with a handful of wildflowers, which she had picked from the meadow beyond the backyard. It was dinnertime, but both women were at home. A few years back, Millie had hired a young woman, who had some culinary training, to help in the kitchen and in running the place.

"We need to start working less and living more," Millie had told Maggie. "We'll work the lunch shift and help prep the dinner and then leave it to the young folks."

Raymond had quit a few years back, with plans of, "Bumming around Europe as the spirit moves me." After he left, it was never the same.

Maggie told Millie, who was at the sink filling a vase with water, about Johnny's death. "John and I would like to pay our respects."

"Of course," Millie said as she turned off the water and looked over her shoulder at Maggie, standing at the kitchen table with her hands on the back of a Windsor chair—one of four Maggie had bought for the house at a yard sale more than a few years back. "So sorry, Maggie. Take all the time you need."

Maggie was absentmindedly running her hand over the top of the backrest, one segment of her mind remembering the huge smile plastered on Millie's face when Maggie arrived home with the chairs.

"Thank you …" Maggie said, half-listening, as an image of Millie, still smiling big, plopping right down in one of the chairs, had appeared. "It's called a comb-back Windsor, you know," Millie had said, sitting back, her bright eyes holding Maggie's. "You are the best of friends, Maggie, the best."

Maggie hadn't seen a smile like that from Millie in years. Ever since Daniel had moved away, that slow but discernible flagging of the spirit seemed to gain momentum on Millie. She could still run the restaurant efficiently, but that joie de vivre had been missing, as though she were going through the motions of work and her life. And in a way, Maggie felt the same.

"John is going to meet me in Bethesda day after tomorrow," Maggie said, "and we'll go from there."

"Before you go," Millie said as she placed the stems of the bluish-purple flowers in the vase, "I'd like to talk with you about something."

The red-eye flight from Los Angeles to Dulles Airport gave Maggie time to process not only Johnny's death but the last eleven years since John departed for Philadelphia. Just as Mr. O'Connor had assured, John had taken full advantage of his educational opportunities at Penn. He had graduated with honors in both undergraduate work in the school of engineering and then a master's degree in architecture from the School of Design.

For the last five years, John had worked at an upscale architectural outfit in Philadelphia and had recently told Maggie of his plans to start his own firm with two other associates from his current company. Like a dutiful son, John came home to Empire Springs every Christmas and one week in the summer.

Maggie missed him terribly but refused to travel east, until now. She filled the void with cooking competitions, including a first prize at the Autumn Festival in Gliberville. Her winning entry was bacon-wrapped chicken with peppery greens and warm pomegranate drizzle—a main course dish had been added to the competition. That was a thrill, as was the article in the local paper about the champion chef, Maggie Meyers, and with a picture of her holding the trophy. That trophy was validation that all her years of learning her craft were not for naught.

Maggie was now fifty-eight years old, and though there were a few pounds added here and there, she still drew an admiring eye from time to time.

But the local men had given up on Maggie years ago, as she had made it tacitly clear by her lack of reciprocal interest. There had even been rumblings of Millie and Maggie being a gay couple. When Millie first told Maggie, they were on the back patio at Millie's house sharing a bottle of Cabernet and watching the sun set behind the hills off in the distance. Maggie had laughed so hard she thought she had cracked a rib. "Of course, we must be gay," Maggie said between laughs. "Why else would we have no interest in the local male population."

Millie's news for Maggie was life-altering. She was going to sell the restaurant and move to Astoria, Oregon, to be near Daniel, his wife, and two girls, ten and twelve. Daniel and his family visited Empire Springs every Thanksgiving or Christmas, which rotated from year to year. Daniel was now over forty, and Millie had recently turned seventy. Millie had asked Maggie if she was interested in purchasing, but she declined.

Every time her family visited, Millie would revert back to her old exuberant self, laughing and cracking jokes with one and all, as she played cards or board games with her grandkids, and reminisced with Daniel about *back in the day*. And when John was there visiting, it really was like back in the day.

And for the last two Christmases, Millie even let the restaurant run itself for three days, while insisting that Maggie do the same. And then when her family left, it was as if a huge vacuum had sucked all the life out of Millie. It was also hard on Maggie when John left after a visit, but Millie's disappointment was etched on her face, a face that was now showing its age with crisscrossed wrinkles that seemed to grow more pronounced each year she said goodbye to her family.

And along with Millie's flagging spirit, the restaurant had lost its verve. Maggie remembered what Millie had said Maggie's first year in Empire Springs: "I installed round tables throughout the restaurant; everyone can face each other, which promotes conversation, which promotes energy—a restaurant needs energy." But to Maggie it had always been more than the tables; Millie had promoted the energy to the place with her force field personality, which seemed to have been deactivated.

Maggie couldn't imagine working and living in Empire Springs without Millie. She was her only true friend. Yes, she had plenty of acquaintances from the restaurant, but Millie was her rock, her anchor in this long phase of her life.

Much to think about, Maggie thought as the plane made its final entry into the dawn's early light at Dulles.

Maggie had reserved a rental car, and by the time she arrived in Bethesda proper at the intersection of Old Georgetown Road and Wisconsin Avenue, she was stunned at the change. She had not been home in thirty years and was amazed by the size and breadth of the buildings. What used to be a town of buildings a few stories high was now teeming with massive structures of concrete and steel.

She had reserved a room with a suite in downtown Bethesda. John was taking the train down tomorrow morning and then the Metro into Bethesda, a block from the hotel. After checking in, Maggie took a two-hour nap and then decided to walk around town. On the corner of Wisconsin Avenue and East West Highway, where the Hot Shoppes used to be, was a massive building that gobbled up the entire corner space. And where McDonald's Raw Bar used to be on Old Georgetown Road, with its one-story brick façade, was a row of bulging concrete structures.

One thing Maggie found still standing was the Tastee Diner, a few blocks north from where the Raw Bar used to be. It still had that shabby retro look with its tacky purple and white window awnings and the purple canvas canopy at the front door. Inside was exactly as she remembered: stools at the front counter, booths along the windows, grizzled guy working the grill, and, of course, the smell of greasy fried food. She took a seat at the counter and ordered "SOS with home fries."

The Tastee Diner was located in a section of town called the Woodmont Triangle, which appeared prosperous, with small businesses and international restaurants and an assortment of bars. Though a couple of high-rises and parking garages had been added, some of the original buildings remained. There was a hum of energy to this formerly sleepy place, which wasn't all bad. *Grow or die,* Maggie thought as she walked back to her hotel down the north end of Wisconsin Avenue; many of the old-time buildings were still standing with new businesses.

Maggie stopped across the street from where the Bethesda Movie Theatre used to be. It seemed pretty much the same, the box office and marquee still standing, with a new name: Bethesda Cinema and Draft House.

Farther down, Maggie spotted Pumphrey's Funeral Home, which was around when Maggie was a child, where tomorrow she and John would undoubtedly meet many of Johnny's old friends at Johnny's wake. Maggie hadn't contacted anyone about her arrival.

Well, she thought, *they'll see me soon enough.*

CHAPTER 42

The following day, after a late breakfast, Maggie drove north on Wisconsin Avenue, which turned into Rockville Pike, past the National Institute of Health on her left with security gates at the entrances. The campus was crammed with new buildings, and off to her right was the Naval Medical Hospital, or Navy Med, as Maggie knew it by. Again, a security gate, and with marine guards at the entrance and an imposing security fence around the perimeter of the grounds. So different from when both facilities were open to anyone: Maggie used to cut through the maze of roads in NIH, and in high school she and Nora would sneak into the movie theater at Navy Med.

After all these years, she still remembered her way around Bethesda. Continuing north on Rockville Pike, over the Beltway and a left onto Grosvenor Lane and a couple more turns, and on her right was Walter Johnson High School. An addition had been added, but the rest of the property looked like the WJ she remembered. Maggie parked on a side road bordering the football field. She walked around the end zone and into the stands where she had sat the first time she had laid eyes on Johnny O'Brien. That childhood moment had altered the course of her adult life. It had ushered in a man whom she loved like no other, a man who provided a heartache like no other, and a man whom she shared a son with, a son whom she loved like no other.

It was early October, and there was a hint of autumn in the air, the leaves just beginning to turn, and it was a day much like this when Johnny O'Brien *click-clacked* in his cleats up the stadium steps in his scuffed and soiled uniform. As he neared, Maggie was struck by the vitality, the charisma, and the life force that radiated from him, radiating from those piercing dark blue eyes. No one could take their eyes off of him. It seemed at once so long ago and yet so near.

Back in the car, Maggie crossed over Democracy Boulevard and into her old neighborhood, Ashburton. There were some new homes and many of the originals had been remodeled, but it still had that look that reminded her of her youth. This wasn't an especially affluent neighborhood that Maggie grew up in, brick ramblers and modest ranch homes, like the one she parked in front of.

Her old home had a For Sale sign out front, and the house appeared empty. The yard needed mowing, and the house looked in need of fixing up: loose shingles, peeling paint, and a general empty tiredness about the place, as though it had run its course.

By the time Maggie returned to the hotel, John was waiting for her in the lobby. After both took a long nap, followed by dinner, they changed clothes for the wake and walked the three blocks over to Pumphrey's Funeral Home. On the way over, John said, "It seems I was only meant to know him in my dreams." He was wearing a dark suit, and it crossed Maggie's mind that she had never seen John's father dressed up—always in work clothes or something casual—coat and tie was not Johnny's way.

When they entered the foyer, the funeral home had a long line of people waiting to sign the registry book. Maggie didn't recognize any of them. After signing, they entered a large rectangular-shaped room with a sea of people conversing in muffled voices. Everyone dressed in black, gray, or navy—the men in suits, the women wearing conservative dresses or blouses and slacks. Off to their left, along a wall, was an open casket. *Oh my god*, Maggie thought. She glanced over at John and he too had noticed. "I have to go over there, Mom," John said. "I don't want to, but I have to."

Maggie took her son's hand in hers, and together they headed for the casket, Maggie avoiding eye contact with anyone. She needed first to get through looking at Johnny's corpse.

An elderly couple was standing over the casket, the woman, with thinning white hair pulled back tight in a bun, leaning on a walker, and the man slight and frail, looking as if a breeze could blow him over.

John and Maggie waited until they turned and shuffled off. "Finest neighbor any man could ask for," the old man said with a glance up at Maggie, who shined a smile on the old gent, and then she and John moved over for a look.

"Just like he looked in my dreams, Mom—just like." John voice was a whisper of awed reverence.

Johnny O'Brien looked angelic to Maggie, with a youthfulness that belied his age, sixty-one by Maggie's count. The dark hair was full with speckles of gray on the sides, and the chiseled face still so handsome. The eyes were closed and the lips slightly parted as though ready to offer some quick-witted line or comment. There he was, her Johnny boy, the love of this life lying in repose after all these years.

"Maggie?"

Maggie turned at the sound of a voice she hadn't heard in years, a friendly voice. She turned to see Johnny's best friend, Danny McKenzie, standing before her. He was much the same, though older, of course, with some age in the face, but still tall and broad-shouldered. "Hello, Danny," Maggie said. If there was one person she needed to see at this moment, here he was, a good guy, Danny.

Danny's face dropped as John turned his attention from the casket. "Oh my God," Danny said as he squinted a look at John as if to make sure he was seeing correctly.

A group of men similar in age to Danny were moving en masse toward Maggie.

Johnny's boys hadn't changed all that much. Like Danny, they were older and many gray, some balding, but they still were a formidable group with that big-man athletic aura they had always carried with them. They were like a younger version of Brent O'Connor.

"Well, well," Maggie said through an emerging smile, "if it isn't the boys from Bethesda I've heard so much about."

It was one of those moments where everything was a swirl of intersecting activity—the boys hugging and greeting Maggie and at the same time gaping in wonderment at John, a living replica of Johnny.

Maggie offered a hand to John. "I would like to introduce my and Johnny's son, John O'Brien."

Hands were shaken and more hugs exchanged. "John, you're the spitting image of your father," Danny said.

After Maggie gave a sanitized version of the last thirty years of her life, and while the group was marveling over John and at the same time recounting old stories about Johnny, Danny pulled Maggie aside and said, "Tomorrow, I want to take you to Johnny's house and show you something."

By nine, the funeral home was empty save Maggie, John, and Danny, who said, "All the boys are over at Rock Bottom Brewery."

Maggie looked at her son. "You go, John."

"Why don't you come, Mom?"

"Tired, John, very tired." she said. "You go with Danny."

Maggie walked back to the hotel by herself. It had been a long and trying couple of days with the funeral still on the docket.

Back at the hotel, Maggie changed into her nightgown and got into bed, leafing through a Bon Appétit magazine. It was still early evening in California, and her body clock had not adjusted yet. Unable to concentrate on reading and with an edgy tiredness hanging over her, she turned off the lamp on the nightstand.

Maggie tossed and turned for most of the night, running through her mind the *what-if* game. What if she had told Johnny about John, and he had offered to marry her and move to Empire Springs? What if Johnny adapted to Empire Springs and started his own landscape business? Mr. O'Connor would have surely helped with recommendations—he would have loved Johnny; everyone did. John would have lived for the first thirty years of his life knowing his father, and Johnny his son. What a pair the two of them would have been.

Or what if Johnny had been miserable in Empire Springs, their marriage an uncomfortable affair with Johnny feeling trapped thousands of miles from his beloved Bethesda and his boys? Or what if Maggie had acquiesced and moved with John back to Bethesda, living in Johnny's mother's house, and she being the one feeling trapped? And would she then have taken John back west, leaving a wide chasm of heartache and distrust between her and Johnny? Could Maggie and Johnny have ended up hating each other?

Finally, in the wee hours of the night, Maggie drifted off into a deep sleep.

As light slipped through a crack in the heavy-fabric drawn curtain, Maggie awoke from a dream so real that she glanced around the room to make sure she was alone.

Johnny had come to her, sitting on the edge of the bed, his eyes shining with life. He was in jeans and a flannel shirt and was wearing a pair of work gloves. Atop his head was a raggedy ball cap, with a tumble of his black hair spilling out from underneath the bill.

"Maggie," Johnny said in a soft whisper. "It's all good. You'll see." He then kissed Maggie on the cheek and smiled his magnificent smile.

Maggie checked the hotel clock, ten thirty. She hadn't slept that late in years; of course, it was three hours earlier in Empire Springs. She peeked into the living room, where John was stirring, stretched out on a pullout sofa. "Morning, Mom."

"Hungry?"

"Starving," John said as he flipped off the covers and stood. "Danny told me," John said with a what-do-you-say look, "I have to order SOS at the Tastee Diner before I leave; he said it was my father's favorite." John made a squinty face at his mother. "He said you'd tell me what SOS stood for."

Maggie and John walked to the Tastee Diner. They sat in a booth in a back room. After they ordered, John told Maggie about going out for beers with his father's friends. "What a group of guys, Mom."

Maggie saw the scene of her waiting on them at the round table in the middle of the back room, trading good-natured barbs, Johnny smiling big, his laugh filling the room with bonhomie. "Aren't they though," she said. "They're my boys from Bethesda."

"Yeah," John said as he leaned back as the waitress placed two coffees down, "they told me all about you waiting on them at the Raw Bar."

Maggie poured a splash of cream in her coffee and lifted her spoon and held it. "Those guys, especially your dad, lit up the room."

"They still do," John said.

Two orders of creamed chipped beef on toast arrived. Maggie thanked the waitress and made a face at John—*Well?*

John made a face back—*Yeah?*

"Shit on a shingle, John. SOS."

By the time they returned to the hotel, Danny was waiting in his car in the drive in front of the hotel. John told Maggie he needed to get his cell phone from his room, so Maggie got in the front seat.

"John tells me he had a great time last night," Maggie said.

"It was like being out with a younger version of Johnny," Danny said. He turned to Maggie, his eyes seeing long ago. "It wasn't just the looks but the mannerisms, and he has that … You know what I mean?"

"Yes, he, like his father, has that indescribable something that draws people to him."

"Exactly," Danny said. He nodded, his eyes busy in thought, and looked off before looking back at Maggie. "You look great by, the way, Maggie. You really do."

There it was in Danny's eyes, that looked she hadn't seen from a man in a good while now—that *I would like to get to know you* look.

"So, Danny," Maggie said as she slid her right hand down to the seat control lever and moved forward. "Tell me about yourself, the last thirty years."

"Two kids, boy and a girl, both grown and out of school." Danny gripped the steering wheel with both hands as though to steady himself. "Their mother died two years ago from ovarian cancer."

"I'm so sorry, Danny," Maggie said with meaning.

The snapping clack of the back door opening broke the moment. "Sorry to hold you up," John said as he slipped into the backseat behind his mother.

Danny threw a look at Maggie, a *to-be-continued* look.

"Had SOS at the Tastee Diner, Danny," John said.

Danny looked at John in the rearview mirror and nodded. "Well?"

"Loved it and the diner."

They drove over to Hempstead Street and Johnny's house. It didn't appear to have changed at all, a little white box of a home nestled under a weeping willow tree, the yard blanketed in a coat of green grass and neatly spaced flower beds along the front of the house.

Danny escorted Maggie and John inside, which looked to be from a time warp from the past—beige wall-to-wall carpeting in the living room-dining room, which was only separated by the variation in outdated furnishings. Maggie half expected to find Mary O'Brien in the kitchen wearing her smock-apron with tiny red polka dots over her white buttoned-down blouse and gray skirt, stirring a pot on the stove, cigarette between ring and middle finger.

Down the steps to the basement that Maggie had never been in before. "This was Johnny's clubhouse," Danny said as they entered a finished room with bead-board paneling, grouted tile floor. There was an impressive oak bar with a red cedar sign, The Bethesdan, hanging over it, just like she had envisioned when Nora had told her about it. It looked like a cozy tavern.

At the rear of the space, next to the sliding glass door to the backyard, was an easel covered by a drop cloth. "Johnny got interested in painting, and like everything else, it came naturally to him," Danny said.

Danny removed the cloth, and there was a painting of Johnny and a boy who looked like John, both wearing baseball gloves, a ball in midair between them—John, his arm extended in a throwing motion, Johnny, his mitt extended to receive the ball. "Johnny told me he had dreams where he was playing catch with a son—Johnny Junior."

All three exchanged silent looks.

"I had the same dream," John said.

"Oh my God," Maggie said as she leaned in to the get a better look. "Oh my God!"

"There's more," Danny said.

"More?" Maggie said, not certain what else there could be.

"I am executor of Johnny's will," Danny said. He then offered his hand to a round table with four sturdy chairs. "Let's sit down."

It turned out that Johnny had willed his estate, including the house that was paid for free and clear, to Maggie. If she wasn't found within a year, it was to go to Catholic Charities. "You made my job a lot easier, Maggie," Danny said.

Maggie's dream flashed in her mind of Johnny telling her, "It's all good, you'll see."

John told Danny about the time he spied on the Fourth of July picnic and saw Johnny with the pretty woman and two young children.

"That's was Carol," Danny said. "She wanted to marry Johnny, and he adored her kids, but he told me, 'She isn't Maggie. None of them are Maggie.'"

Maggie sat there staring at Danny unable to utter a single word.

"You were his once-in-a-lifetime girl."

CHAPTER 43

On the way back to the hotel, Danny said, "Maggie, I'd like you and John to come to my place for dinner tonight." They were at a stoplight on Old Georgetown Road in front of what Maggie remembered as Brown's Store, a clapboard A-frame, with a triangular sign atop the porch: Bethesda Community Store.

In Danny's gaze there was a *please say yes* look.

John leaned forward, his head between them. "If it's all right with you, Mom," John said with a tap on Maggie's shoulder, "I think I'll head back to Philly."

Maggie turned and looked back at her son, and she saw all that she needed to know. "If that's what you want, John, it's fine by me." It had all been a lot for John to take, seeing his father, or more exactly his father's corpse, for the first time, in a casket, meeting with Johnny's buddies, hearing the stories. He needed to return to his life in Philadelphia and digest it all. And attending the funeral did seem like an after-the-fact thing. But Maggie was staying; she would see it all through, including dinner at Danny's, which she was looking forward to, really looking forward to.

After Danny dropped Maggie and John off at the hotel, John soon departed for the Metro station, and Maggie had the remainder of the afternoon to kill before Danny picked her back up.

Back in her room, Maggie called Millie and filled her in on the events up to this point. And then she added, "I'm having dinner at

Johnny's best friend's house tonight—Danny McKenzie is his name; he's a widower."

"Ah-hah," Millie said. "What's he's like."

"Steady-as-you type of man, nice-looking, and John told me he's his kinda of guy."

"Well, do I smell a romance?"

"I feel so comfortable with him, like it was just yesterday instead of thirty years ago that we last saw each other."

"Take your time, Maggie. Katie has things under control at the restaurant," Millie said in reference to the young chef she had hired to ease the burden on her and Maggie. "She's like a younger version of you."

"But without the baggage," Maggie said with a laugh.

From the hotel, Maggie crossed Wisconsin Avenue and headed south before turning west on Bethesda Avenue to a foliage-lined upscale section of six-story condominiums constructed of steel, brick, and glass: boutique shops; and restaurants with bright-colored awnings and outdoor dining areas with matching umbrellas. All of this years before had been an industrial district. She purchased a bottle of cabernet for dinner with Danny and peeked in and out of the sleek, expensive shops. This was not the old Bethesda crowd from the Raw Bar, but affluent, sophisticated people dressed in expensive dresses or casual chic, some of the men in top-end jeans and expensive, trendy sneakers. Everything about this section of Bethesda reeked of money and education.

In a women's clothing store, Maggie saw a beautiful jade-green knitted sweater. It was not cheap, but for the first time in years she was going to dress for a man tonight and decided to treat herself.

Back at the hotel, Maggie took a shower and then blow-dried her hair in the mirror, wearing a plush hotel robe. She decided to put her hair in a ponytail, like she used to do when she was younger—she had always worn it in a ponytail when she waitressed at the Raw Bar.

Maggie studied her face in the mirror, a few lines extending out from the corner of her eyes, but her skin still had that lovely honey-gold hue and with a trace of a glow in the cheeks. Part of her felt like a teenager getting ready for a big date with a guy she wanted to impress. Something had transpired between Maggie and Danny, ever since that moment in his car when he said, "You look great by, the way, Maggie. You really do." They had looked at each other, and in their eyes they were speaking a silent coded language of reconnection and admiration. It was a mutual *I would like to get to know you* look.

Maggie decided on a pair of corduroy pants and tennis shoes to go with the knitted sweater. After dressing, she returned to the bathroom mirror and not only did the sweater feel great on her, but Maggie had to admit she looked rather stunning in it. The jade-green color set off her olive skin and her glimmering big brown eyes and the finely sculpted bone structure. "Nice to see you again, stranger," Maggie said to her reflection in the mirror, before heading for the door.

Outside the hotel, Danny was standing at his car parked right where it had been earlier. "Maggie, you look fabulous." He nodded as if to confirm his words. "The fabulous Maggie Meyers."

Maggie smiled so big, she could feel her eyes squinting. "Thank you, Danny," she said as she handed Danny the bottle of wine she had purchased. "Hope you like cabernet."

"Absolutely," Danny said as he inspected the bottle of wine. "Good bottle of wine with a beautiful woman." He offered a roguish grin, and opened the passenger door. "Has anybody told you lately, Ms. Meyers, you are one fine-looking woman?" He nodded as if to answer his own question and then offered Maggie a crooked salute.

Danny's house was in Johnny's neighborhood. "It's my parents' house that I recently bought from the estate when my mother passed," Danny said as he pulled into the driveway of his home, a brick colonial. "Johnny's handiwork," he said as he offered his hand to the well-manicured lawn, mulched flower beds, and neatly trimmed shrubs in the front. "After my wife died, I just needed to live elsewhere."

Danny's living room had a gas fireplace emitting an amber glow to the space. Maggie and Danny sat in comfy chairs facing each other. Danny opened Maggie's bottle of wine and poured two glasses on the coffee table. He lifted his glass and said, "A toast to old friends lost and found."

Maggie clinked Danny's glass and took a sip. "Oh, that's good wine." She sat back and nestled herself into the big, soft chair. It felt good to be in the company of one of her boys, a man who was the best friend of the love of her life, a friend who was making clear his interest in her. Not just the words, but in that silent coded language they were speaking to each other, each with a remembering look, a look of finding a surprise gift from the past. Not since Johnny had she felt this comfortable with a man.

Danny told Maggie about his life: "Accountant for the federal government, retired after my wife died—probably a mistake." He leaned forward to refill their glasses. "If it wasn't for Johnny," Danny said with a faraway look and a shake of the head. He looked at Maggie and nodded. "He was always there for me, always."

A silence fell over the room, a silence draped in old memories.

They exchanged looks and reconnected to the moment at hand.

"So tell me, mystery girl," Danny said as he refilled the wineglasses. "Tell me about your life."

There was something so pure and sincere in Danny's words, a tremor of understanding as though he had intuited there were some rough patches along the way. "After Johnny and I broke up, I left Bethesda for Mexico with the wrong guy ..."

Maggie went on to tell Danny every detail of her time in Mexico, including the murders and her near rape and death.

Danny reached over the coffee table and took Maggie's hand in his. "I always thought of you as courageous."

He squeezed her hand, and she put her free hand over his. "You were always a good listener, Danny."

Maggie then told about her life in Empire Springs, the birth of John, cooking competitions, and her love life. "I had some relationships and flings along the way, but none of them was Johnny."

They were still holding hands, and neither seemed ready to let go.

"I loved Johnny like a brother," Danny said. "He was there every step of the way during and after my wife's illness, from coming by the house to making a meal to having a few beers after work." Danny laced his fingers through hers. "Something I'd like to show you, Maggie."

In the dusky autumnal light of early October, they walked the three blocks to Ayrlawn Rec Center. "It looks the same," Maggie said as they stood on a small rise looking down.

Ayrlawn was a long and wide expanse of grass, nearly big enough to hold two full-size football fields. In a corner off to their left, there was a backstop, and at the far end another, even larger, backstop; across the field, an asphalt basketball court, and next to the basketball court on a raised area was Ayrlawn Elementary School.

The sun was setting over a line of trees at the far end. It was so quiet and still—not a whisper of wind or a sound of a car or another person, as though the moment was meant for Danny and Maggie. "I come down here sometimes," Danny said.

Maggie reached for his hand, and he slipped his fingers through hers and once again it felt so right.

"Sometimes I can hear Johnny's laugh echoing in my mind when I stand here." Danny turned to Maggie. "Do you remember his laugh?" He said it more as a statement.

"It was musical."

Danny turned and faced Maggie. "I know I'll never be Johnny, but something has happened between us these last few days."

Later that evening, Maggie called Millie. "Had a great time at Danny McKenzie's home—drinks and dinner and a stroll down memory lane."

"You sound *sooo* happy, Maggie."

"So do you, Millie."

"I'm going to come back to Empire Springs, pack up, and drive cross-country back to Bethesda."

"Looks like we both found ourselves new lives, Maggie."

"Let's have a big going-away party for the both of us."

"As the new owner of the restaurant would say, 'Abso-fucking-lutely.'"

"What?" Maggie screamed. "Are you telling me Raymond is back?"

"Brent O'Connor is putting up the money on one condition."

"Let me guess," Maggie said. "Raymond has to put the yurt back up on the O'Connor property."

"It's all falling into place," Millie said with a trace of nostalgia in her voice.

"Do you remember what you said to me all those years ago when I first came to Millie's Place?"

There was a momentary silence before Millie cleared her throat and said, "I do—this is the beginning of a good, long friendship."

"Millie?"

"Yes, Maggie?"

"We were a helluva team. Weren't we?"

Our Lady of Lourdes was standing room only, and with a full choir seated behind the altar. Maggie sat in the front row with Danny, the rest of Johnny's friends, and their wives in the two rows behind them. It was a Requiem Mass and was a long service, but to Maggie there was something spiritual about it. She could almost feel Johnny's presence when the choir sang "Libera me," a song that was also sung at her father's funeral. There was a haunting power to the voices that seemed to fill every section of the church from the sacristy to the nave and overhead to the ceiling.

After the funeral, there was a luncheon at a local restaurant in Johnny's honor, and during the serving of coffee and cake, Danny stood and asked for everyone's attention. He removed some folded papers from inside his jacket pocket and studied them for a moment. "I spent a long time trying to put down on paper ..." Danny looked off for a moment and said, "But I think it best if I speak extemporaneously." He folded the papers and returned them to his pocket and then smiled. "I can almost hear Johnny saying, 'Ah, Danny, how about keeping it simple and say *off the top of my head.*'" A murmur of laughter erupted.

"I first met Johnny O'Brien in the summer of 1956 at Ayrlawn Rec Center, and by the end of that day and until the day he died, we were best friends. Over all those years, I never remember us having a disagreement of any magnitude."

Danny then talked about Johnny's generosity and loyalty, offering a few examples. "Johnny never considered life to be about how much money you made, but about the people you touched on the journey."

And in closing, Danny said, "I will always remember Johnny, all of us boys, at Ayrlawn—the football practices, the hoots and hollers of rambunctious boys at play. In the autumn the smell of leaves burning in the street wafting down onto the field, our growing bodies straining to outdo each other."

Danny cleared his throat and seemed to steady himself. "And never will I forget his laugh that never, ever grew old." Danny exhaled deeply, his eyes seeing long ago. "I'll always remember Johnny that first time we met, his eyes shining, his endearing smile spread across his youthful, handsome, young face, such an endearing smile." Danny looked over the audience, nary a dry eye in the house, and said, "Go gently into the night, Johnny, my boy—go gently."

It came over Maggie that she had come full circle. That she had been running from Johnny's memory, and his death had brought her back to where she belonged—back home with one of her boys from Bethesda.

Printed in the United States
By Bookmasters